Sisters Eleanor and Mary St. Aubin have
used their combined wit, social connections
and determination to create a living for
themselves as professional matchmakers.

The St. Aubin and Briggs Confidential Agency
in Bath prides itself on discreetly matching ladies
and gentlemen in need of a marriage partner.

To catch the eye of an eligible suitor, their aspiring
brides-to-be need the most exquisite dresses
around. Only the finest garments from renowned
modiste, Sandrine, will do!

These three ladies have made a business
helping others find their matches.
What happens when they meet their own?

Find out more in

The Earl's Cinderella Countess
Their Convenient Christmas Betrothal
How to Court Your Wife

All available now from Harlequin Historical!

Author Note

Thank you so much for joining me on this journey with the Matchmakers of Bath as they search for their own HEAs! I loved bringing together so many of my favorite things—visiting Bath, helping others find true love and, now, with Sandrine, fashion! It can have such a transformative, artistic effect, and it changes Sandrine's life.

I've loved clothes ever since I used my grandmother's quilting scraps to make gowns for my Barbies. I loved color, pattern, texture and, most of all, I loved how different Barbie could be depending on her outfit. I was making my first characters! She could be romantic, glamorous, serious, funny; she could fade into the background or be the standout in the room. Just like Sandrine, and the ladies she helps with her work. She builds confidence and joy, and finds that again with her long-lost love in the bargain.

You can visit my website, ammandamccabe.com, anytime to read more about my Behind the Book research!

Until the next book!

HOW TO COURT YOUR WIFE

AMANDA McCABE

Harlequin

HISTORICAL

If you purchased this book without a cover you should be aware that this book is stolen property. It was reported as "unsold and destroyed" to the publisher, and neither the author nor the publisher has received any payment for this "stripped book."

Harlequin® HISTORICAL

ISBN-13: 978-1-335-83154-5

How to Court Your Wife

Copyright © 2025 by Amanda McCabe

All rights reserved. No part of this book may be used or reproduced in any manner whatsoever without written permission.

Without limiting the exclusive rights of any author, contributor or the publisher of this publication, any unauthorized use of this publication to train generative artificial intelligence (AI) technologies is expressly prohibited. Harlequin also exercises their rights under Article 4(3) of the Digital Single Market Directive 2019/790 and expressly reserves this publication from the text and data mining exception.

This is a work of fiction. Names, characters, places and incidents are either the product of the author's imagination or are used fictitiously. Any resemblance to actual persons, living or dead, businesses, companies, events or locales is entirely coincidental.

For questions and comments about the quality of this book, please contact us at CustomerService@Harlequin.com.

TM and ® are trademarks of Harlequin Enterprises ULC.

Harlequin Enterprises ULC
22 Adelaide St. West, 41st Floor
Toronto, Ontario M5H 4E3, Canada
www.Harlequin.com

HarperCollins Publishers
Macken House, 39/40 Mayor Street Upper,
Dublin 1, D01 C9W8, Ireland
www.HarperCollins.com

Printed in U.S.A.

Amanda McCabe wrote her first romance at sixteen—a vast historical epic starring all her friends as the characters, written secretly during algebra class! She's never since used algebra, but her books have been nominated for many awards, including a RITA® Award, Booksellers' Best Award, National Readers' Choice Award and the HOLT Medallion. In her spare time, she loves taking dance classes and collecting travel souvenirs. Amanda lives in New Mexico. Visit her at ammandamccabe.com.

Books by Amanda McCabe

Harlequin Historical

The Demure Miss Manning
The Queen's Christmas Summons
"His Mistletoe Lady"
in *Tudor Christmas Tidings*
A Manhattan Heiress in Paris
"A Convenient Winter Wedding"
in *A Gilded Age Christmas*

Debutantes in Paris

Secrets of a Wallflower
The Governess's Convenient Marriage
Miss Fortescue's Protector in Paris

Dollar Duchesses

His Unlikely Duchess
Playing the Duke's Fiancée
Winning Back His Duchess

Matchmakers of Bath

The Earl's Cinderella Countess
Their Convenient Christmas Betrothal

Visit the Author Profile page
at Harlequin.com for more titles.

Chapter One

1811

Don't stare, Sandrine. Do not stare!

Sandrine Jaubert was very stern with herself, turning over the strict admonition in her mind as if she was her old governess, Mademoiselle Verdy. Mademoiselle had been wonderful in teaching Sandrine the joys of drawing and painting, the beauty of fashion and art and needlework. But she'd never had much luck turning her dreaming, distracted charge, who would just rather be sketching or following her father around his fabric warehouses taking in all the colour and texture, into a proper, sophisticated French lady. Much to her exasperation. And her remembered scoldings didn't help Sandrine now.

She just *had* to stare. She could not help herself.

Tucked away on a quiet corner of the Comtesse de Fleurieu's ballroom, she had a better view through the swirling crowd, the sea of bright silks, pastel muslins, feathers and jewels, than those in the thick of the crush could hope for. She usually found such nooks and hidey-holes at parties, spots behind potted palms and in window seats with draperies, where she could watch the parade of fashions and dream up her own designs to sketch later. Where she could let the twirl of colours and shine flow over her without drawing talk and laughter, and the knowledge that she could never be quite good enough in this world. Could never be what her parents so longed for.

Sandrine sighed sadly to think of *that look* in her mother's eyes when she examined her only child, of that shake of her father's head when Sandrine stumbled in a dance or laughed too loudly or not enough. It was always Too Much or Not Enough.

The Jauberts had come from respectable but certainly not *gratin* families back in their native France, fleeing to England after the Great Terror. It was only through the disaster and tragedy of what was happening in their homeland that they built great wealth in London. They'd fled the revolution with toddler Sandrine and a few trunks of coins, jewels, and blueprints for their secret manufacture of a particular kind of silk, along with the accumulated knowledge of their business from generations past. Sandrine's mother, Marie-Claude Jaubert, was known as a great beauty, and as someone who had longed to be received at Versailles and have a grand title in her youth, she had quickly set about finding paths into higher society in their new homeland. She'd succeeded beyond most other's dreams, and her husband made an even greater fortune as a result. Now she wanted to be accepted in more ballrooms like the Fleurieus', great, ancient titled French families keeping their standards in this strange new world.

A daughter of the 'right sort'—beautiful, witty—would have helped immensely. Instead, they only had Sandrine.

Sandrine glanced in a gilt-framed mirror hanging on a nearby wall. Not tall, not short, with chestnut hair rather than a fashionable gold, and a few freckles on her nose that were the bane of her life. And she was not witty, at least not aloud. Her thoughts of the world around her, of human foibles and eccentricities, often made her giggle, but only to herself. Mostly she wanted to hide away in her little studio room, painting and drawing, imagining new, beautiful worlds. She loved her mother's tales of the beautiful fashions of her French youth, how it made the women look like goddesses, and Sandrine longed to capture such things for herself. Then she could forget everything else, and be only what she wanted to be.

A lady in a pale green and silver gown floated past Sandrine's hiding place, shimmering in the candlelight, the glow catching on the tiny gold beads in the skirt's tulle trim. Sandrine adored the colour of the lustrous satin, how the changeable shade made the wearer's complexion glow like the evening sea. But she didn't quite approve of the cross-over bodice, which did not suit the lady's willowiness. It would be better in a simple scoop, a bit of that tulle draped over the shoulder, perhaps. She slid over a couple of steps to more closely examine the beadwork, nearly toppling over the brass pot of a towering flower arrangement.

As she grabbed at the wobbling arch of white roses and lilies, she glimpsed her mother in the crowd. Marie-Claude was clearly looking for her disappearing daughter, her lace fan impatiently flapping, a little frown between her sky-blue eyes.

Sandrine quickly ducked back into her hiding hole—and that was when she saw *him*. And she really could not stop staring that time.

She shivered, even though she felt flushed with heat—the terrible curse of her milky-pale skin was the inevitable rush of red-sun warmth that poured down over her whenever she was embarrassed or anxious or shy or scared, as she was far too often. She feared she was quite crimson now as she stared in frozen silence at the man who now stood in the ballroom entrance, directly in her line of sight as if the crowd had magically parted for him, the chandelier light falling directly onto him making him appear to glow.

She felt as if she'd been plopped down right in front of her favourite place for sketching, the classical galleries at the British Museum, before the most gloriously sculpted figure of an ancient god. Tall and powerful, he quietly commanded the room without even a movement or word, without even raising one elegant hand.

His gaze, some pale colour so luminous it was piercing even at a distance, swept over the crowd almost as if coolly indifferent, completely serene, and Sandrine imagined he was just gracing mere mortals with his blindingly beautiful presence for a moment before flying onward. Yet somehow she sensed he *did* look for something among that sparkling kaleidoscope, his study lighting on one object then another, until a tiny frown of something like disappointment took its place.

If only he looked for *her* in that way. What a dream that would be! But then again, whatever would she say if he *did* talk to her? It would be as if that museum god-statue had suddenly come to life and said something to her. She would freeze utterly.

The Comtesse de Fleurieu, their hostess, hurried to him with a brilliant smile, and he moved at last, half-turning to greet her. Some of the light Sandrine had imagined surrounding him shifted into shadow, and a bit of the dizzying magic shifted and transformed. She studied the details of him. Unlike a Greek god, he wore fashionable garb of a beautifully tailored dark blue and shimmering ivory waistcoat, a simply tied but impeccable cravat fastened with a small cameo. His glossy, dark, curling hair was a bit too long, and tumbled over his brow to be flicked impatiently from those astonishing eyes. A smile, just a very small one, touched the austere line of his lips, but it was utterly transforming. It looked like mischief, humour, conjured out of indifference.

A burst of giggles from beyond her hiding place pierced a bit of that sunlit, hazy dream that had come over her. She glanced over to see two young ladies, clearly of that confident, popular sort Sandrine could never be, fashionably dressed in pink muslin and blue silk, blonde curls bouncing, fans waving as they whispered behind them.

'...really is *him*!' one of the Giggling Girls said. 'They did say he would attend this evening, but I didn't dare believe it. Oh, don't stare so, Rosemary! What if he sees us? I shall faint away.'

'If only he *would* see us,' Rosemary moaned. 'My cousin said he's been gone from London for ever so long, travelling, but she saw him riding at the park yesterday. Riding with a *lady*, in most close conversation.'

'Are you sure it was a *lady*?' the first Giggling Girl said with a—yes, with a giggle. 'He had the most scandalous reputation before his parents sent him away from Town. Gambling, racing, and—and fast women.'

'No! Shocking. And his family so very grand. Much older than our own Royal Family,' Rosemary whispered. 'But my cousin did say this particular lady was dressed most respectably. Even rather unfashionably. Perhaps he has mended his ways. Perhaps he is looking for real romance now. There is nothing so splendid as a reformed rake.'

'Oh, Rosemary, you were always such a swoony goose! He is *French*. They are not romantic in that way at all.' GG number one tilted her golden head as she watched the ancient god nod and smile at their hostess. 'But it's true I've never seen anyone quite so handsome in real life...'

Neither had Sandrine. And now she so longed to know who he really was. A Frenchman of a grand family! A rakish Frenchman, freshly arrived from some mysterious absence. Who could he be? A prince? A lost royal? She thought of some French princes whose portraits she'd seen—pasty, long-nosed, balding *monsieurs*—and she rather thought not.

Surely her parents must know of him. Her mother was an expert on the aristocracy of their homeland. But Sandrine did not, for she was quite sure she'd remember him well.

'The d'Alencys might be ancient,' Rosemary said, rather wistfully, 'but they say their fortune was quite lost in France, and they must struggle so sadly. And his mother was a niece of the Noailles! How tragic.'

'I doubt my father would even approve of such a suitor for me, then,' the first Giggling Girl said with a sniff.

'As if he would ever look at you twice, anyway.'

They moved away in an outpouring of quarrelsome words, and Sandrine lost their flow of gossip.

He was a d'Alency, related to the Noailles. Sandrine gasped, and parted some of the concealing flower arrangement for another peek. Of course she'd heard of that family. Ancient *noblesse d'épée,* they served the kings at Versailles, fought in wars, were cardinals and counts. Everything her mother adored from their old home, their old world.

When Sandrine was a child, she'd often placed her dolls, dressed in gowns of her own design and carefully stitched together herself, into tales of adventure she could never imagine for herself, conjured from paintings she'd seen of France. Battles, courtly halls made of gold, gardens filled with fountains and the scent of roses, people of unimaginable beauty and dignity and daring. If she'd known of this d'Alency with the beauty of a god, he would have featured in those tales very heavily.

Oh, yes, she was certain now she would melt into a puddle on the parquet floor if he spoke to her. He was a dream-figure. She could never have conceived of a more romantic, heart-stopping tale in her old doll theatre.

He was not at all the sort who would think twice, or even once, about someone like her. She was too petite, too pale, too shy, their families not of equal rank at all. Yet she feared she would drift away entirely up into the clouds to dream of him. She had a dizzying vision of suddenly rising off her feet, floating across the room to his side, transforming on the way to an elegant, fashionable beauty who would dazzle him with her glow...

She took another step to the side to try and get a better view. As if he sensed her intense study, he suddenly glanced over in her direction. Sandrine's heart pounded, as if it would rise up in her throat and choke her, and her cheeks burned. She started, and the brass flowerpot clattered, the flowers swaying precariously as if it would all topple over and seal her humiliation. What if *this* was his image of her, not the elegant sophisticate she longed to be but the clumsy girl who knocked over flower arrangements?

She snatched at a branch of greenery and kept it

from tumbling down. That pale, otherworldly gaze drifted over Sandrine entirely, and she dared take a breath. He hadn't seen! She had a chance to collect herself and find a way to make another impression!

But then his attention snapped back to her, and his eyes narrowed, the dark, stern line of his brow lowered. In—disapproval? Disdain? She held her breath, waiting for that split-second of regard to pass over her, perhaps to the Giggling Girls. To her shock, it lingered.

His gaze flickered over her, down to the very tips of her satin slippers then back up to the pearl bandeau in the upswept waves of her chestnut-brown hair. The very corner of his lips twisted, in a sort of smile that transformed the austere lines of his face once more into mischief, and might have seemed almost improper in someone else. But not him. No, in him, it somehow seemed very different, an invitation to join in some secret mirth, some joke between only the two of them. He gave her a small nod, and their hostess tapped his sleeve with her fan and drew his attention away.

Sandrine was utterly frozen in place, as if *she* had become the statue she imagined him. She longed to laugh, to spin in a giddy circle, to feel *everything*, if only she could move. She'd lost her precious hiding place, though. The Giggling Girls had paused their exit to watch her, and worse, her mother had spotted her.

Marie-Claude hurried towards her, like a grand sailing ship on the ballroom sea, parting all before her in her topaz-coloured satin and flashing diamonds. She took Sandrine's arm in a firm, even pinching grip, as if she feared her daughter would slip away again. Which was silly; Sandrine had become adept at hiding, but not yet at escaping after being seen. Through a dazzling, albeit gritted smile, Marie-Claude drew her daughter back into the thick of the crowd.

'There you are! I have been looking everywhere for you, *chère fille*,' her mother said. 'I have told you many times, you must not drift away to dream all the time. It was not an easy feat to gain the invitation to the Fleurieu ball; we must make the most of every moment. You are almost twenty now. It's past time for a match, a fine marriage I have worked so hard to prepare you for now. You must remember that, Sandrine.'

'I always remember that, Maman,' she murmured. Of course she always remembered that. It was constantly before her. All the lessons, the governesses, the gowns and hats and jewels, they were to raise her family in the world.

'Lord Everington wanted to dance with you, and was much disappointed you could not be found to accept. His title is not French, of course, but his mother is from Bordeaux, a very fine family.'

Lord Everington was fifty, a widower with three children, and had almost no hair left atop his head. Sandrine fervently hoped her mother's dreams of grandeur wouldn't come at such a price.

Marie-Claude suddenly brightened. Sandrine never trusted that certain gleam in her mother's eyes. It always meant some kind of trouble for her, such as talking to men like Everington. 'But no matter now! I just saw the arrival of Monsieur d'Alency, heir to his father, the *comte*. Perfection indeed.'

There her mother was certainly not wrong. He was lost to her view now as they made their way through the crowd, but she would never forget the glow of his eyes, the shadowed angles of his glorious face, the little smile he'd given her. But she also remembered what the Giggling Girls had said—he had such rakish ways. 'The one who gambles and races?'

'Ah, you see! Even you have heard of him, from the depths of your paintboxes. His family is *noblesse d'epee,* back to Louis IX.' And that was what her parents longed for the most. Ancient nobility.

Sandrine, though, knew she would want only *him*. Only to know the secrets behind those beautiful eyes, the heart under the rogue. 'But we are tradesmen, Maman.'

Marie-Claude scowled and pinched her daughter's arm just above her glove. *'Ferme ta bouche!* Not here in England. We are *French*. And we can help the d'Alencys, if they would let us. They lost their lovely châteaus and fine jewels long ago.' She glanced at Sandrine, frowning a bit over her hair, not golden as it should be. She smoothed her pearl-edged white muslin sleeve, straightened her necklace. 'No matter the state of their finances, though, they will certainly care about the appearance and character of a young lady. Style and deportment are always of greatest importance in a French lady.'

'That takes me quite out of their attention, then,

Maman,' Sandrine said. Her looks and clothes were only barely above average, and she knew it well. Though if her parents were to let her leave off the simple whites and pastels of a girl and dress herself as she really wanted to, it might be different.

Marie-Claude suddenly swung Sandrine around to face her, holding tight to her arm. 'That is enough of that,' she whispered fiercely. 'I have worked far too hard for too long to see you ruin everything, Sandrine. I raised you to be a grand lady, to take a place in Society both here in London and once we can return to Paris. You owe me, owe your father.' She narrowed her eyes as she studied her daughter carefully. 'You are a pretty girl, a *belle jeune fille*. If you would just know that, remember that, and make the most of it. Smile. Flash your eyes, they are such a nice blue. Pay little compliments to gentlemen, be interested in their interests.'

Interested in cricket and cravats? Sandrine couldn't quite make herself do that. Cravats, yes, of course; sport, no.

She thought of the beautiful Monsieur d'Alency. He must have many more deep thoughts than about cricket. 'Surely I would have to be Aphrodite herself to gain such a man's attentions,' she whispered.

'Don't be ridiculous,' her mother scoffed. 'I told you, you are *French*. That is all that is needed.' She reached out again and straightened Sandrine's triple strand of creamy pearls fastened with diamonds and rubies, grander than what most debutantes had but still perfectly tasteful. And perfectly expensive. 'And you have a fine dowry, thanks to your papa and your grandmother. Do not forget *that*, either.'

As if Sandrine ever could forget that. Her parents' house was filled with reminders in every painting on the silk-lined walls, every piece of porcelain and silver, every Aubusson rug, every slipper and fan and bracelet.

'Now, come along, *chérie*. We haven't much time.' Marie-Claude spun Sandrine around and marched her forward again.

'Time for what?' What she really wanted to do was go home and get out her sketchbook, make an outline of that godlike face before she lost the details. It was nearly the hour she was allowed to depart.

'Our hostess has agreed to introduce you to Monsieur d'Alency.'

Sandrine's footsteps came to a skidding halt. She was to actually *meet* him? Stand close to him, look into his eyes, and be expected to say actual words? To be polite, interesting, elegant, to smile? That horrible hot-cold flush came down over her again, and she trembled. 'Maman…'

Her mother frowned down at her. 'What now?'

'I'm not ready for such a thing,' she whispered. 'I don't know what to say or do.'

'What to say?' Marie-Claude laughed. 'Have we not been educating you for such things all your life? Art teachers, dancing masters, the pianoforte and harp, the best modistes and coiffeurs! You have been perfectly prepared to meet people, to take your place among Society. It is *facile*.' She snapped her fingers as if charm and grace could be turned on just like that.

Sandrine glanced around desperately. She saw so many women who seemed to have that confidence and grace so easily, laughing at their partners' jests, waving their fans in lazy arcs, sparkling and dazzling. Her mother was right, of course, she'd been taught such things as long as she could remember. But being admired and poised, marrying well, leading Society in fashion, was harder than any lesson book could ever convey. She'd read of so many French ladies in past centuries who had led salons, influenced art, been beautiful and elegant; women of style, wit, unique spirit. How she admired them! How she longed to be like them, and not at all like herself. Not shy and blushing.

And surely it all started with finding a man of equal spirit and dash. Surely, if she could somehow manage to do that, if such a man admired her, she could become what she yearned for. What her parents so wanted.

The crowd parted a bit, and she caught a glimpse of Monsieur d'Alency, laughing with their hostess, shaking back that curl of glossy hair with a careless little gesture. He was like a dream come true. Dashing, energetic, handsome beyond compare, filled with that air of confidence that couldn't be faked. Could such a man pay attention to her, *see* her? Was it even possible?

There was only one way to go now—forward. Towards him. It wasn't possible to run, even if she did feel all tight and breathless, as if she would faint. Her mother held on to her too tightly, the crowd packed too close, and she had to take a chance now.

Besides, she told herself sternly as she stood up straighter, held her head higher, it was only an introduction. A curtsey, a smile, a hello. Just one tiny moment.

She nodded, and her mother's grasp loosened. They made their way towards the Comtesse de Fleurieu and the god. Sandrine hoped with all her might that her pasted-on smile wouldn't crack her face. She curled her free hand into the lace overskirt of her gown to keep it from shaking.

'Ah, Madame Jaubert,' the *comtesse* said. 'How lovely to see you again! And your delightful daughter. May I present one of our own countrymen, and my godson, Monsieur d'Alency? Alain, this is Madame Jaubert, and her daughter, Mademoiselle Sandrine. They are originally from Lyon, I believe, though sadly have been forced to live here in London like the rest of us for many years.'

'Madame Jaubert, how do you do?' he said, and his voice was exactly as Sandrine would have imagined it. Rough and rich, deep as brandy, touched with a musical accent. He bowed over her mother's hand, making even Marie-Claude blush. 'Lyon is indeed a beautiful place, or so my father has told me, with the glorious hills and the waters of the Rhône.'

Marie-Claude seemed to melt. 'It is the most beautiful place in all the world, if I do say so myself, monsieur. I grew up there, and it is where I found my dearest husband and had my beautiful daughter, though she has no memory of it at all.' She tugged Sandrine closer, and didn't seem to notice when Sandrine stumbled a bit on her slipper.

'Mademoiselle Jaubert. Such a great delight to meet you.' He took her hand, balancing her gloved fingers on his as delicately as if she were made of glass. She didn't blame him for being rather careful, for she had the most powerful urge to grab him and pull him close, to inhale his delicious scent of lemons and something like cinnamon.

He looked right into her eyes, seeming to peer down to the very core of her. So close, she saw his eyes were actually grey. Not a plain, taffeta-fabric grey, but the grey of a roiling, stormy afternoon, always shifting, changing, sometimes revealing shades of pale blue, drifting into dark night. For an instant, all she could do was stare up at him, captured by those unique colours, the spark of light that flashed through them as if sharing a joke. Something did seem to be hidden behind that beauty, some depth underpinning his careless demeanour. His mask-like looks hid some secret she wanted desperately to know.

Everything else around her blurred and vanished.

How she would love to draw him! That face, with its sharp angles, impossibly high cheekbones, the straight blade of his nose and the severe line of his brows, contrasted with the tumble of curling hair and soft lower lip, was endlessly intriguing. If she just shaded a bit here, sketched a line there...

A tiny smile quirked at the corner of his lips, a mesmerising dimple flashing low in the smooth, light golden colour of his cheek, making him seem even more intriguing.

Sandrine suddenly realised what that lightning-flash of amusement must mean. She was staring! Gawking, like a ridiculous, gauche schoolgirl, and he was amused by her. She longed to sink into the floor, out of sight.

Her mother surreptitiously pinched her arm, and Sandrine forced herself to look away. She dropped a quick curtsey. It wobbled rather precariously, but at least she did it. He squeezed her fingers, the lightest touch, yet it felt like a flash of sparks from her fingertips all the way through her, making her glow all the way down to her toes.

She gasped, and her gaze flew back to meet his before she could stop herself. His smile widened, and she was again struck by that vivid contrast between his classical statue-like exterior and that quick, fleeting glimpse of pure sunlight.

How she longed to shout out that no, she was not really a complete featherbrain! She *did* know how to speak, to have manners. It usually didn't just fly out of her completely. Only when she was faced with a flare of pure, sizzling magic. Only with him.

But she could only curtsey again.

He let go of her, and she had to resist the urge to

shake her fingers. To curl them in and hold on to that touch.

'Alain,' the *comtesse* said. 'I am longing for a nice, cosy chat with Madame Jaubert. Perhaps Mademoiselle Sandrine would care for a stroll to the refreshment room? Or a little peek at my *petite* conservatory...it is quite my great pride. I love the jasmine; it was transplanted from Versailles itself and the smell is heavenly! I understand the *mademoiselle* is a very gifted artist, and she might enjoy sketching them soon.'

To walk with *him*? Be alone with him? Well, as alone as one could be in such a crushing party. Something fluttered with excitement, or maybe fear, deep inside her. Surely, maybe, free of her mother's close study, she could relax, find a way to be more of herself with him? To learn more about him, his secrets. Memorise his ever-changing face for her sketchbook.

'Yes, certainly,' he said politely. He held out his arm. 'Shall we, Mademoiselle Jaubert?'

'Thank you, *monsieur*. I would love to see the conservatory.' Steeling herself not to jump again as if startled by a clap of thunder, Sandrine slid her gloved hand into the crook of his elbow, feeling the strength and tension of his muscles under her touch.

She sensed the beaming gaze of her mother and the amusement of the *comtesse* as they made their way around the edge of the party, towards the open door leading to the conservatory. She glimpsed the two Giggling Girls, staring with open-mouthed astonishment as they passed. She would almost have laughed at their reaction that she, unobtrusive little Sandrine behind the potted plants, was with this dashing god-figure, but she was much too astonished at it all herself. How quickly the evening had changed completely! From boredom, longing to escape, to tingling, sparkling excitement.

She peeked up at him, at the angle of his profile, his perfect nose, the wave of his hair. He glanced at her out of the corner of his eye, and smiled again.

Her gaze snapped ahead. 'If you have friends to meet, *monsieur*, I can certainly make my own way amid the plants. I know my mother and Madame Fleurieu can be quite like a runaway carriage at times—it's hard to refuse to move along with them.'

That smile widened again. 'A runaway carriage?'

'Yes. You cannot turn it no matter how you try, so you must find a strap to cling to and go with it wherever it takes you.'

He laughed. *Laughed!* It was so warm and rich and alluring, a fire on a cold day, bittersweet chocolate. 'I promise, *mademoiselle*, I am an excellent driver, and I can turn a carriage whenever I wish it. I'm always hoping to escape a crowded party whenever possible, especially in such pretty company.'

Sandrine's cheeks flamed again, and she ducked her head to try and hide it. He'd called her *pretty*! Surely he said so to many ladies, but she could hardly dare believe she'd heard it. 'You don't enjoy parties, then?'

'Not such loud, overheated ones, I confess.'

'Why do you attend?'

He tilted his head to look down at her, his pale eyes

hooded. 'For much the same reason you do, I expect. Because my parents said I should.'

Sandrine laughed, too. Not a demure little giggle, but a full outburst she couldn't hold back. It felt bold, freeing. The whole thing was not quite as scary as she'd feared. 'You let them take the reins, then?'

'As you say, *mademoiselle*—sometimes one must just hold on and enjoy the ride. My parents are certainly the team in harness together who insist on being heard.'

Sandrine sighed. 'As are mine. Fighting against it only makes the ride last longer...'

'And the crash worse.'

She wondered if this moment would end in disaster, if his little jokes and smiles would carry her heart quite away. Maybe it would be worth the ride indeed. 'Sometimes, yes.'

'But not tonight.'

His smile shifted, changed, became almost—kind. Could it really be? 'No?'

'No. Tonight I get to escape the party with the loveliest lady in the room.'

Now he *was* being kind. Or maybe even making fun of her. Sandrine pasted on a stern expression. Whether he was a Greek god or not, she wouldn't be laughed *at* by him. Not unless she meant to be. 'With someone like Miss Petrie around? And Lady Martin-Stokes? They say she is quite the acknowledged diamond this year. I am merely an—an opal, I think. Maybe a garnet, on my best days.'

He laughed louder, longer. How she liked that laugh! How it drew people in, made them feel giddy themselves. She feared she could get too used to it. Too addicted to it. 'But opals are certainly very dramatic. Such hidden depths and flashes of fire. You never know what you're going to get with an opal.'

Hidden depths and fire. Just what she thought of him. 'I did hear you had a roguish charm, *monsieur*.'

A frown replaced that smile, a flicker of solemnity. He looked away. 'You shouldn't listen to all gossip, *mademoiselle*.'

'I seldom have the chance to listen to any at all. My life is too quiet, my friends few. But Maman would be shocked at how much someone can hear hiding behind potted plants at parties.'

They stepped through the glass doors into a new, magical world. Sandrine gasped at the sight that greeted her, so unexpected and different from the elegant white and gold ballroom. Warm, damp air, smelling heavily of jasmine and roses and greenery, swept around them, and the noise of the party was muffled, far-away. They were not entirely alone; whispers and laughter echoed from other strolling couples, hidden behind the green-draped aisles, but she saw none of them.

She drifted into the gravelled walkways lined with shelves and plants, every shade of green from palest jade to blue-green emerald. Splashes of brilliant yellow and crimson flowers, reaching to the glowing glass ceiling, spread everywhere.

'How astonishing,' she whispered. 'Oh, I wish I could find every shade of green in here at Care & Barnhalt! But I don't think I could ever capture the way this very air shimmers. Maybe with an alla prima technique?' She mused on to herself, forgetting she was supposed to be an elegant, witty, aloof Frenchwoman and just being a painter, lost in images.

'You are an artist?' he asked, following her down another aisle lined with heady lilies.

Sandrine leaned down to examine a delphinium, and realised it looked rather like his eyes, shading from palest aquamarine at the centre to near-black at the edges. 'Oh, no. That is, I like to draw and paint, to imagine new ways of seeing things around me. But I am a mere scribbler, no true artist. I haven't been at all properly trained.'

'New ways of seeing?'

'Of course. Don't you ever imagine things *better* than they are? More beautiful, more—more vivid?'

'No, never,' he said, a bemused note in his voice. 'Perhaps I should.'

She glanced back at him. He was studying her closer, as if she was a new creature he'd just discovered, as if he was trying to fathom her. Flustered, she turned away, and pointed at a delicate purple and cream orchid. 'Look at this.'

He leaned close to her, his sleeve brushing her arm, that lemon-herb scent of him enveloping her until she was dizzy. 'An orchid?'

'Not just an orchid, rare as those are. See this shade

of colour here, this line that divides it in perfect symmetry? All perfect, without artifice. It's glorious! It makes me think of the twilight sky, makes me feel like I am in a different place just looking at it.'

'Yes!' he said in delight. 'How right you are. Just like a sky, streaked with gold into purple and blue and white.' He looked at her, a wide, real, beautiful smile on his face. 'What a most unusual lady you are, Mademoiselle Jaubert, to see so much in a little flower. The world must be filled with magical colours for you. You must see so very many things the rest of us can't, see below the surface to the truth of things. You must never let that go.'

Sandrine stared up into his eyes, so close to her own, now a clear, cool grey. He looked back, as if he could really see her. Finally, someone did! Someone understood.

And that was when she fell headlong, utterly in love with Alain d'Alency.

Chapter Two

Alain shouted in wild delight as he gave his horse, Gallia, his head, the two of them flying free together over the open fields outside London. He'd left his friends far behind, winning their impromptu race as he usually did, jumping ditches and fences as easily as snapping his fingers.

Yet winning a race was not the point, never the point, even with his best friends. Just being free for a few precious moments *was* the point, forgetting everything but the cold snap of the wind, the open spaces all around, the laughter that couldn't be held back. He had a small space where he was just Alain, just whatever he wanted to be, whatever he felt in his heart. No ancient titles, no expectations, no always-watching eyes, gloomy rooms crowded with ghosts that lingered over every hour, never loosening their icy grip. They held him and his sisters tight, no matter how they wished to be free.

Alain had always had a longing to travel, to prove himself, to make his own fortune. Be his own man, see what he could do. Now any chance to fulfill those burning dreams seemed further away than ever.

Here, outdoors, the old past, the old expectations, were gone, lost in a blast of light and fresh air and speed. He could never outrun it, never completely lose being a d'Alency, but he could lose sight of it for a time, hide from it, pretend there was something else out there. Pretend there was freedom.

He felt the tightening of Gallia's powerful, sleek muscles beneath him, the split-second anticipation, and they were airborne. Sailing up, up, up into the wind and soaring over a fence. Alain shouted again with the joy, and imagined he could fly up, dream-like, into the clouds themselves.

They landed, light as one of those very clouds, and he tugged at the reins to turn them onto a different path, carefully slowing their headlong dash. Gallia tossed his head, his raven-dark mane rippling, as if he too felt the glory of flight.

Gallia was a horse who loved his freedom, who didn't like taking orders—much like Alain himself. It was what had drawn Alain to him that day at Tattersalls, the way he'd looked into Gallia's liquid-brown eyes and seen a fellow wild spirit. It was why the price for him had been actually one Alain, with his pockets to let, could afford. It took a while to persuade Gallia to follow some direction, but now they could move as one. He sensed the lightest touch to his reins, the lightest press, and trusted enough to follow Alain's lead.

As they moved into the dappled shade of the tree-lined path, everything turned to a shimmering stillness around them like a fairy-wood. He remembered what he'd told Sandrine Jaubert at the ball, that he was always in control of any runaway carriage.

He laughed to think of her now, of the way she saw tiny things around them like flower petals, shades of green, how unexpected she was. His parents told him he must go to the *comtesse*'s ball, no matter how much he would rather go to play at cards at one of the small, secret clubs tucked behind Mayfair. They told him he must meet certain young ladies, with an emphasis on Mademoiselle Jaubert.

'The family's lineage is—*plein de regret*,' his mother had murmured as his father mentioned Sandrine Jaubert. 'In France, it would never have been considered.'

'Yet they have prospered in this English world of ours,' his father said sternly, pausing to cough into his handkerchief. 'The d'Alencys have always been of a practical turn of mind, *ma chère*. We must be even more so now.'

Alain's sister, Catherine, had secretly rolled her eyes, making Alain want to laugh, but they had both stayed silent. What use had arguing with his quiet, elegant, implacable parents ever been? The Comte and Comtesse d'Alency were always scrupulously correct, perfectly mannered, and utterly immovable. If they said he must attend his godmother's ball and meet certain young ladies, he had to do so.

But he could be perfectly correct as well, do what

they asked, and not go a step further. He knew what they intended next, had always intended since he had toddled around their modest new London rooms, far from the family château. An advantageous marriage. The d'Alencys, unlike the Jauberts, had not prospered in England after fleeing bloodshed and mayhem in France, leaving everything behind but their lives and their fine name.

But Alain had his own ideas, his own image of the future. He longed to travel more, seek out adventures, meet new people, build his own fortune, make a small home one day with someone he loved. Soon he would have to make some decisive turn. In the meantime, a few dull parties, a few pleasantries to pretty young ladies, could do no harm. His parents had indeed been through many horrors in life, and he wanted to make them happy if he could. For now.

But he hadn't been expecting Sandrine Jaubert.

He'd never met the Jauberts. Though they lived in similar worlds—namely the French emigre world of London—Alain's mother preferred to keep to her own small circle of old friends. Aristocrats who lived in the memories, preserving the old ways as much as they could. It was only of late, when it had become clear how very unsustainable things were really becoming, that Alain's father, the *comte*, stated they must expand their sphere to French businessmen, or, horrors, even English ones. Hence the Jauberts and their extensive textile holdings.

His mother's friend, his own godmother, Madame

Fleurieu, who had escaped France with her own portable wealth and built it into havens for fellow emigres, suggested a ball. She would find young ladies of fine dowry and respectable, though not high-born, families, and thus enable Alain to meet them in festive and informal settings. Examine them, though the words went unspoken. Just like a horse sale, but not nearly as much fun.

'It will be easy, Celeste, you will see,' Madame Fleurieu had murmured soothingly to Alain's mother when the *comtesse* began to weep softly. 'Alain is so handsome, so charming, he will not have the tiniest trouble finding a wife who will be quite enthralled with him. She will be easy to mould into the proper sort of wife, and soon you will have grandchildren to carry on the d'Alency name! As well as the means to live as your name deserves.'

As if to emphasise her point, a chunk of crumbling plaster fell from the drawing room ceiling to crash on the faded carpet. His mother wept even harder.

So Alain had an image of Sandrine in his mind, fair or not. Plain, awkward, silent, grateful, steered by her own parents.

And it was true that at first she was not the most socially assured young lady he'd ever met. At first, she seemed so painfully shy she could barely look at him. She trembled as if she stood in a cold windstorm when he took her hand. Yet she was certainly not plain. Her soft, chestnut curls set off a peachy-fresh skin that went from pearly-pale to sun-touched red with a blush that surged and ebbed as if to reveal every thought. Small and slim, with a high, small, ivory decolletage framed in beaded white lace, pearls glowing in her hair and at her throat, she looked like a wood sprite, a fluttering nature-creature. He half expected her to sprout gossamer wings and flutter up out of the ballroom.

He was fascinated against his will. She was really almost *too* expressive, too exposed, with those blushes and tremblings, and he had the most powerful urge to warn her to be more careful. To keep her emotions well-hidden from the talons and tearing teeth of Society before they tore her wood-sprite heart away. To keep the core of herself hidden from everyone, as he did.

Then she looked up at him, and he found himself staring into a pair of glowing, jewel-green eyes that went right to the centre of everything. He knew then that she possessed some deep strength, one that probably even she didn't know about. He started to dare to hope. If she could see him, the real him, perhaps she could understand. Could *know*. Maybe they could help each other.

His hope they might be friends, that she could understand, relate, only grew as they talked amid the green serenity of the conservatory. Her light humour, her artistic spirit, it drew him in. When she looked at him, she really *looked*. She seemed to glimpse what he hoped to be, not his name or his face or the romance of his family's tragedy.

She had her own passion, he could tell; a passion for

art. It was a part of her, that colour and light. Maybe she, too, longed for freedom, to pursue that art without the expectations of family hanging over her. Maybe she would understand if he told her of his dreams.

He came to a small clearing, just before the path left the wood and turned towards the road back to London. Alain paused there to wait for his friends. He tilted back his head to stare with a dawning sense of wonder at the way the buttery-yellow sunlight filtered through the late-summer leaves, turning their tips gold. He'd never noticed such things before, dapples of light and shadow, colours and line. It had to be from seeing the lush greenery of the conservatory through Sandrine's eyes, hearing her speak of the beautiful world that lay just beyond everyday notice.

Alain thought the spot reminded him of his school days at Lycée St André, a small establishment in Kent established by Monsieur Aurac, another French emigre who had once taught royal princes and *ducs* and now instructed the children of his exiled countrymen. It was a refuge behind its impeccable white walls, run as closely as Monsieur Aurac could along the lines of *Ancien Régime*, a replacement for home and family.

Now those schooldays were far behind, and he had to find his own path. But one thing from St Andre always haunted him. Danielle. It had been thus since they were barely more than children.

Danielle Aurac was the granddaughter of their schoolmaster, a rare beauty, a lady who had the pure, ivory, classical cameo face of a Renaissance princess in a Fra Angelico painting, and of equal serenity and mystery. Ever since Alain first saw her on his arrival at school, he'd been lost. She seemed so kind, so gentle, so adored by everyone, and as they grew older the feelings only blossomed. And, miracle of miracles, she seemed to feel the same about him.

At first, when he left school and decided he should seek some career, he dared hope that one day they could come together. He would build his own fortune, make a home for them. Surely, once his family had settled more into their English life, they would be charmed with Danielle just as he was, and they would see how such a future could be made.

His love had blinded him back then. Danielle had no money and his parents would not give up their old ways, their old dreams; he could not go into trade, not find a career to support himself and Danielle. The *comte* and *comtesse* would not countenance such a thing.

Hope had faded slowly, though, when it was all he could hold on to, all he had. They wrote to each other, reassured each other in wild, fleeting hopes that a solution would be found. Now the first glimmer of a new, bizarre, daring hope was taking shape—an alliance with Sandrine Jaubert where they could help each other. It could not be perfect, could not be what they once longed for, but it was a way he and Danielle, and Sandrine too, could gain much of what they wanted.

Alain, tired and pensive after his ride, turned down his parents' street as the sun was beginning to slide from the sky, leaving streaks of lavender and gold behind in that quiet moment before the evening's theatre performances and balls began. They wouldn't be happy he was so late; his mother had told him at breakfast they were invited to cards at the home of the Marquise de Brillac, and he could not be late. The Marquise had once been lady-in-waiting to the queen herself, and such connections had to be carefully maintained. But he could not quite care, he had so many other things to consider, plan.

Gallia was moving as slowly as Alain himself after the long day of escape amid the sun and fresh air. To be free after the shadows and unhappiness of his family's home was always exhilarating. But now the wide sky was receding behind the small townhouses in their identical rows, the shuttered shops, the overgrown patches of garden.

He saw as he came around the corner that he need not have hurried anyway, for his family wasn't alone. An elegant dark blue barouche, far grander than any usually seen in the neighbourhood, complete with uniformed coachman and footmen, drawn with stunning matched greys, sat outside the d'Alencys' door. Alain drew up to study it for a moment, just as their neighbours did from behind their front windows. The house's door opened, and Alain's mother, the *comtesse* Celeste, appeared with a stout gentleman in an old-fashioned wig and fine, bottle-green superfine coat.

His mother seemed so small, almost bird-like next to him, so dainty in her plain blue muslin dress and high-piled, silver-streaked dark hair, her head held high, a small, reserved smile on her face. The man beamed down at her, speaking quickly, enthusiastically as she gave the littlest of nods. She held out her hand, the long, pale fingers adorned only with the sapphire ring once gifted to her ancestor by Louis XIII, and the man bowed over it.

The *comtesse* watched, perfectly still, perfectly expressionless, as he climbed into his fine carriage and that magnificent equipage sailed away, leaving the street as quiet and nondescript as before.

Alain waited until the door closed behind his mother before he moved, taking Gallia to the stables at the end of the street. He was still in no great hurry to return home, for he was quite sure that man, his strange visit, had something to do with *him*. That something was sliding beyond his control, something was about to change.

As he stepped into the small hallway, with its chipped tile floor and unfashionably dark wallpaper, everything seemed silent. The drawing-room door was closed, the evening light from the high, dusty windows hazy.

'Psst! Alain.' A whisper floated down from the narrow staircase that wound its way up from the left.

He glanced up to see his younger sisters peeking down at him from between the banisters: Catherine, who had been a baby when they left France and was now a young lady of rare, delicate, porcelain-like beauty, and Francoise, the surprise arrival after the d'Alencys settled in England. She was only thirteen, and should surely be asleep in the chamber the two girls shared at the top of the house. But, as usual, she had to follow Catherine wherever she went, and Catherine had to know everything that was happening.

Alain looked to the closed door, and heard nothing beyond it. He hurried up the stairs to sit beside his sisters.

'It looks as if we had a caller,' he said.

Catherine slid closer to him, resting her golden head on his shoulder. She was so very pretty, so intelligent and curious, she deserved something better than their shabby house, their small circle. 'For the last two hours at least. We didn't get to meet him.'

'He had such a lovely coat,' Francoise sighed. She always pored over the fashion papers, yearning for silks and bows. 'I wish I could wear such a green!'

'And he had a *yellow* cravat,' Catherine said, mock-swooning at the horror. 'I was shocked Maman let him through the door!'

'She must have a good reason,' Alain said.

Catherine glanced away, fidgeting with a fold of her white muslin skirt. 'I wouldn't know...'

Alain gave her a nudge. He feared he knew all too well what that reason was. 'You know *everything* that goes on everywhere, Cat-kins.'

'It was Monsieur Jaubert,' she whispered. 'He came to call about you, of course.'

That was quick work, but not so surprising. Alain had just met Mademoiselle Sandrine, though he knew he shouldn't be too surprised. Madame de Fleurieu would no doubt have reported all about last night to his mother. It was so typical of his parents to disregard his opinions, his desires, sure they always knew best. He swallowed his fury and smiled at his sisters; they didn't deserve his ire. 'No wonder there's no fuss over my lateness this evening. They must have been most engaged in conversation.'

'Indeed. Papa said you would only be in the way, and things should be quickly settled,' Catherine said. 'That was before they closed the door, and we could only hear a word here or there.' She stamped the toe of her faded slipper. 'So unfair! I am not a child now.'

Françoise's grey eyes were huge in her freckle-dotted face. 'Are you *really* to marry that man's daughter? And will we all have such carriages afterwards?'

Alain hugged them close. How precious they were, his little sisters! How much he longed to help them, protect them. Give them carriages and beautiful clothes. His parents knew how he detested the idea of marrying for money, how he wanted to prove his own worth! He could surely look after them all, if given time

But time was not on their family's side at all, he feared. 'You must have heard a *soupçon* more than a stray word or two.'

Catherine and Françoise exchanged a quick glance. 'There are such draughts in this house, you know, Alain. Sound quite carries. Maman has rather changed her tune about people like the Jauberts, hasn't she?'

'Indeed,' Alain murmured. She had used to sob

about their lost home, their lost way of life, and declare that such petit-bourgeois shopkeepers now lorded it over *comtes* and marquises. Now they had to admit they needed those 'shopkeepers'. 'But I think we see why her melody has shifted.'

Catherine tilted her head as she studied him. 'So you *are* to marry Mademoiselle Jaubert?'

Alain thought of Sandrine, of her shy smile, the way her unexpected warmth and sensitivity had unexpectedly drawn him near. 'I'm not entirely sure about that. It is a possibility.'

'But do you even know her?' Catherine asked. 'Can she possibly make you happy?'

Françoise's eyes welled, as if she was about to burst into tears. 'You have to marry a *stranger*? Oh, no, Alain! Not for a carriage!'

Alain kissed the top of her head, an impossibly tender ache flooding through him at how much he loved his sisters, how much he owed them. He felt he was being torn in two, his own longings warring with his duty to his family. 'She's not a stranger, sweet poppet. I met her at our godmother's ball.'

'Was she terrible?' Catherine whispered. 'I hope she did not look like her father!'

Alain laughed, thinking of Sandrine's wood-sprite face and soft, chestnut-gold curls. 'She did not look at all like Monsieur Jaubert, from what I could see. I wasn't able to spend much time with her, but she seemed kind and intelligent. She likes art, and fashion, just as you do, Françoise.'

'But is she someone you would want to marry?' Catherine persisted. 'Someone you could *love*?'

Alain's thoughts flickered to Danielle, how long he had craved her smile, her touch, how just being near her was so filled with sparkling excitement. 'What a romantic you are, Cat. How could I possibly know that about Mademoiselle Jaubert right now?'

Catherine scowled. 'I am not *romantic*. I see how life truly is. We must all survive. But we do see every day with our parents how it is when two people are bound only by duty and convenience. You deserve so, so much more.'

It was true, their parents rarely conversed now, rarely sat in the same room. Their father, his health fading more every day, hid in his library while their mother took tea in the drawing room with one or two old friends. They were united only in their memories, their names. Alain never wanted that, not for himself, and especially not for his sisters. With money, they could find a wider circle, greater matches. They counted on Alain to ensure those things, never talking to him about it, always expecting he would follow their dictates. 'I told you, Sandrine Jaubert seems a very kind, gentle sort of lady. And I'm not at all sure we're to be married, anyway.'

Catherine glanced around at the peeling wallpaper, the chipped banisters. 'I am too young to find a good marriage yet, or so our parents say, so I fear all their hopes are on you. If only I could do this myself! I know

I could find someone with enough wealth for all of us, someone who could take care of all of us.'

'Or me!' Françoise cried. 'I could marry a prince who would take us all to his castle, where it's always warm and there are lots of cakes. And pretty hats.'

Alain hugged them, his heart so full it would surely burst. He owed them anything in his power he could give. No matter what his own dreams were, of travel, self-sufficiency, love. 'No, no. I only want you both to marry men you love, truly and deeply.' And he knew, in that moment, with a fierce certainty, he would do anything at all to make sure of that for his sisters. He would even face a Medusa in her cave.

And Sandrine was very, very far from a Medusa.

The drawing-room door opened and his mother stood there, outlined in firelight. Even on warm evenings, his father needed the flames to keep the ever-present damp away, to ease his aching lungs. His mother looked so small there, so frail and yet so proud in her shabby gown, her plain cap.

'Alain,' she said, in her softly accented voice, impossible to read. 'You're home at last.'

He stood quickly before she could notice Catherine and Françoise lurking there, letting them escape up the stairs. 'Forgive me for my tardiness, Maman. I only need to wash and dress, and I'll be ready in a trice for the marquise's card party.'

She waved this away, her sapphire ring gleaming. 'It is of no matter. Do come and sit with your father and me; we must talk.'

He moved slowly down the stairs, towards the open door, remembering the dreadful tales of his parents' friends marching proudly to the guillotine. He almost laughed at himself for being dramatic, but the look in his mother's eyes sobered him.

His father sat in his favourite, faded brocade chair near the fire set in the small grate, wrapped in cashmere shawls. He had once been a handsome man, indeed the d'Alencys had been spoken of as one of the loveliest couples at Versailles, and his hair was still dark, his eyes a vivid pale blue. But he was thin, pale, the bones of his face sharp through his skin. He spent his days in dreams.

The room was not large, but it was filled with bits and pieces his parents had rescued from better days, porcelain, portraits of ancestors, embroidered cushions. Balanced on a small card table was his mother's most prized possession after her ring, a Sèvres tea set, rimmed with gold, painted with vivid garden flowers. And there was a decanter of wine.

The *comtesse* sat down on a narrow settee across from her husband, and gestured Alain to sit beside her. The room was silent for a long moment, filled only with the crackle of the fire.

'Monsieur Jaubert has just left us,' his mother said. His father stared into the flames.

Alain wished he could have some of that wine. 'So I heard.'

The *comtesse* sighed. 'Catherine. Of course. That

girl would have been such a useful spy for the likes of Queen Catherine de Medici.'

Alain laughed to picture it, despite the heavy atmosphere of the drawing room. Catherine would indeed have been a fine spy, slipping around the château corridors, listening behind tapestries, luring people in with her angel-looks. 'Not her fault; I saw the carriage leaving.'

'You met his daughter, I believe,' his mother said. 'What did you think of her?'

That she was unexpected. That she was a woodland fairy. Under other circumstances, another life, he might have thought of her differently. 'I would hardly imagine it matters what I think.'

His parents glanced at each other. 'We must all do difficult things to protect the family, I fear,' his father said. 'Look at what happened to our friends in the terrible upheaval of our home! I do fear Mademoiselle Jaubert may prove as inelegant as her unfortunate father. When I think of what should have been—the match our son could have made! The Princess Royal should not have been above the reach of a d'Alency! And now...' His voice caught on a cough.

The *comtesse* poured out a glass of wine and passed it to her husband. 'The shame of it all.'

Alain felt a flare of anger for Sandrine Jaubert, who had been so gentle, so sweet. A rush of fury for himself, at having his dreams so disregarded, so ignored. 'She was not vulgar in the least! She was cultured and intelligent. A bit shy, but perfectly mannered.' And pretty, too.

His mother's head tilted. 'You liked her enough?'

'As well as any other young lady in London, I dare say.' She was not Danielle, of course; no one else could be. But Danielle was beyond him now. His own dreams were beyond him.

'That is all for the best, then, for I fear we must receive her, and all her family,' the *comtesse* said. 'We may even have to claim a—a close connection with them. If you agree, *naturellement*.'

As if he had ever had a choice. His life had never been his own, and he knew what he owed his sisters now, owed his name. He had to swallow his pride, find a way to move ahead. 'And I'm sure we will be rewarded well enough for the connection.'

'Don't let their vulgarity rub off on you, Alain,' his father snapped. 'You will one day soon be the *comte*, the head of this family. We have been robbed of our rightful place in the world, but not of our dignity.'

'I am sure Mademoiselle Jaubert will soon learn our ways,' the *comtesse* said doubtfully. 'And we can soon find some country home, somewhere she can live quietly.'

'Where an heir can be produced, a continuance for our line,' his father rasped on another cough.

'So her money will pay for her prison?' Alain gritted out.

His mother shook her head, her eyes closed, as if she was suddenly deeply weary. 'You have been reading those dreadful romantic novels Catherine so enjoys. A pretty country estate is no *prison*. The Conciergerie was a prison. We will all live there, where your father can have the fresh air he requires, and your sisters can prepare for Society. Where we can be free of...' She held up her hand before Alain could argue. 'And yes, the Jaubert dowry will help us gain those things. Will enable our survival. And so we will be kind to her, always.'

Alain's hands curled into tight fists, barely holding back his anger, his burning sense of the unfairness of the situation for all of them, especially the sweet Sandrine. But he knew how the world really worked, knew his mother was right. There was no time for him to travel and try his dreams of earning a fortune. His father was ill, his sisters growing up. They needed him. And maybe, just maybe, he could help Sandrine, too. Give her some room to find her own freedom.

His mother seemed to sense his thoughts, his anger *and* his resignation. For had it not been she, for all his life, who had taught him the importance of duty? She gently touched his hand. 'I know that you love your sisters, *cher*, that you want all that is fine for them, all their beauty deserves.'

'*Oui, Maman,*' he muttered. He did love Catherine and Françoise; he loved his parents, too. He had to help them if he could. He couldn't be careless forever. His dreams of making his own way in the world, making his own fortune—there was not time for them now.

'And you say this girl seems well-mannered, genteel,' she said. 'I am sure we can make her one of us, that we can find a way forward together. I should not wish to ask this of you, but we must. We must beg you now to help us, my son. Help our, *your*, family.'

Alain glanced at his father, so frail now, so helpless, and it felt as if a heavy iron mantel descended onto his back. The past and the future were cut off, and he and Sandrine were left together on the far side of it. He didn't know yet how she felt about it all, but he knew what he had to do. He hoped fervently they could find a way together, an accommodation for them both.

'If Mademoiselle Jaubert will have me,' he said through gritted teeth, 'I would be happy to ask for her hand.'

Chapter Three

Sandrine slipped down the stairs the next morning, bathed and dressed in a new, buttery-yellow gown, with her hair curled and pinned. She fairly skipped, sure that her sense that something hovered on the horizon was true. Something great and lovely was about to happen, to change!

She moved through the grand hallway of the house, scented with fresh flower arrangements, bathed in light from high windows, and moved towards the pale green and gold music room, her mother's favourite room, where the pianoforte and harp waited in splendour. She smoothed her skirt, knocked on the door, and slid inside at her mother's call of *'Entre!'*

That chamber was only used for important moments, with its beautifully fashionable arrangements, its giddily sunlit French paintings of shepherdesses in meadows and forests. Her parents sat under one of those images now, a tea table laid out before them, their heads bent together as they whispered.

'Ah, Sandrine, there you are! It grows late,' her mother said, as if she herself was not usually locked away in her darkened chamber at such an hour. 'How pretty you do look, *petite*! I did once fear you would be my thin, gawky *fille* always, but no, no. Does she not look well, Pierre?'

Her father smiled at Sandrine fondly. He'd always been indulgent of her, kind, though now he didn't have much time for her. 'Our *petite fleur*! You will certainly do us proud.'

Sandrine perched on the edge of a chair across from them, fairly sure she would leap up and shout if she didn't hear what was happening soon. 'Will I, Papa? I have indeed always wished that.'

'Our greatest desire for you is about to come true,' her mother said, beaming on her often-unsatisfactory child, 'thanks to our invitation to Madame de Fleurieu, and your beautiful behaviour there. You showed yourself quite worthy of the *noblesse d'épée*, just as we have worked so hard to prepare you.'

She knew it! It was happening, really happening. It was no dream. 'Do you mean...?'

'Our little *comtesse*!' her father boomed, and clapped his hands.

'He—loves me?' Sandrine whispered.

Her mother took her hand. 'Your papa called on the d'Alencys yesterday, and they were all that is welcoming. It shall all be arranged, if you and young Alain agree.'

If she agreed. Sandrine had to restrain herself from leaping up in joy and running out to order the bridal bouquet. Her throat felt too tight for her to speak.

'Indeed, they were very charming,' her father said. 'I fear their house as it is at present is not all that could be wished for, my little jewel, but that will be remedied soon enough. They were most amicable to my suggestions, once all comes to—'

'Pierre!' Sandrine's mother snapped. 'I did warn you about the correct way to broach such matters to the d'Alencys. Perhaps we are not at home in France now, but that is no reason for improper indelicacy.'

'Indelicacy!' her husband cried. 'If we were in France, *chérie*, I would never have been admitted to their hallway, let alone negotiating a betrothal. There is no time for tiptoeing about this matter. They need us. You should have seen the state of their drawing room! And I must be sure our Sandrine is looked after suitably.'

'Oh, Papa, I am quite sure that Al—that is, Monsieur d'Alency will always look after me,' Sandrine insisted. She knew his reputation, his rakish ways, but surely she'd seen better. Surely she'd glimpsed his true self there in the conservatory. Everything was going to work out now.

Her father pinched her cheek. 'Ah, my sweet flower! Indeed he will, if he knows what's good for him. And I will make sure of it.' He reached for some papers laid out on the tea table. 'We will find you a proper home, a townhouse near by, plus somewhere in the country, and provide you with a suitable dowry. But the money from your dear grandmother, who helped me so much in establishing our business here, that will be yours entirely from the wedding day to use as you must. It will not be the d'Alencys'.'

'Pierre!' Sandrine's mother gasped, her expression appalled. Sandrine was no less shocked. She'd known her grandmother, who had worked with Sandrine's father after they came to England and built her own fortune, had left her a sum that was carefully invested, but surely it wasn't meant to be hers entirely. It wasn't the way when a lady married. 'What must they have thought of such an extraordinary thing?'

Sandrine's father shook his head, his jaw set. 'I hardly care. Sandrine must have some measure of power, or people like that will drown her spirit! You must be able to visit your art-supply warehouses whenever you like, *fleur*, and you shouldn't have to run to your husband whenever you need some new pencils or some such.'

Her mother still seemed distressed by the unconventional concept, and Sandrine was sure Alain would always take care of her, but she knew when her father was unmovable. 'If you say so, Papa,' she murmured.

He smiled broadly and clapped his hands again. 'But you need not worry about it! The money will be waiting for you in the bank. You need only listen to your young *comte*'s proposal when he calls this afternoon, and say your *oui* or *non*.'

'Today,' Sandrine whispered, her head whirling. Who would have imagined a dream could come true so quickly?

'He will come to take you for a drive after luncheon,' her father said.

She nodded. Surely Alain *did* care for her, just as she had hoped. Their life would be started today, their foundation laid. She kissed her parents quickly, and dashed off to prepare for that future to begin.

Sandrine added a shaded bit of Prussian blue to the scene she was painting, or rather trying to paint, and stepped back to examine it with a frown. She always hated it when the mood of a scene, the colour and emotion and movement, did not match what she saw in her head—and it never did. Nothing was ever quite as she longed for.

She tilted her head to study the arc of a cloud and added a dab of violet, a focal point of darker colour, hoping to add some richness. A bit of complication. She didn't want to be a mere ladylike dabbler, as her parents encouraged her to be. Some pretty watercolours, a few competent sketches of flowers, were most acceptable, a lovely ornament. They had even reluctantly set her up a studio in an unused sitting room, where the light from the tall windows was just right, and she could find quiet moments to herself that were elusive in the rest of the bustling house.

But they didn't see how hard she worked to move beyond pretty, pleasing little scenes. How she longed to pour all her emotions, her hopes and fears and dreams, all she concealed behind her shy exterior, onto paper and canvas. To put a colour to her desires, to free those feelings and fly away! On the rare occasions her mother wandered into that room, Sandrine would hide her half-finished canvases and put out her floral still-lifes.

She'd begun the new image of the stormy seascape with such high hopes. The wild sky, the lashing of the waves against the shore, called to something in her. Yet she couldn't quite capture the turbulence.

Perhaps she simply needed to *live* more, she thought, as she so often did in her secret, yearning heart. She'd been stuck in her parents' house for—for always, really. She'd thought life would begin in the future, once she found her destiny. Was it now in view?

Maybe, once she became Madame d'Alency, with Alain by her side, that life would truly begin. She almost twirled around at the thought. It couldn't happen fast enough.

If he asked her. Hope, fear...it was all tangled up inside of her. He hadn't arrived yet, as he'd promised her father he would.

Sandrine, now unable to concentrate on her work at all, pulled a cover down over the half-finished scene and put her brushes aside to clean. She sat down on the old settee near the windows and took out her sketchbook instead. She flipped through the pages of gowns and hats and jackets she'd dreamed up, and found the one she'd begun just after Madame de Fleurieu's ball. A wedding gown.

At most weddings she'd attended, the brides wore very pretty dresses, lacy bonnets, many of the silks and muslins sourced from her father's own warehouses, but they were not *grand*. Weddings were quiet affairs here in England, of course, nothing like the tales she'd heard of French royal and aristocratic weddings. Surely a wedding, that step forward into a new life, that melding of hearts, deserved something really special. Something unlike anything else.

She'd often imagined such gowns, created for characters in favourite poems maybe, or heroines in plays, but now she tried to envision what she herself would want if she was floating down the aisle of a great cathedral.

She studied what she had so far, a train beaded with pearl lilies, sleeves edged with lace flounces, yet just like the painting it wouldn't quite come together as she hoped. She closed her eyes and imagined a church filled with flowers, the glow of stained-glass windows, heard notes of music, and caught a glimpse of a figure cast in sunlight and shadows waiting for her...

Then it all melted away. She frowned down at the pencilled lines, and tried to decide instead whether there should be a longer train, a double sleeve. Could there be lace inserts, or some ribbon embroidery on the bodice edge?

She'd become absorbed in changing the waistline when she heard footsteps on the stairs outside. She had just turned the page from the gown to a scene of a vase of roses when Justine burst in. The usually dour maid looked positively animated.

'Monsieur d'Alency has arrived!' she cried.

Sandrine shot to her feet, excitement, tingling life flooding through her. 'He is here? Now? Oh, I must change my gown! And my hair...' She touched her hair, so carefully dressed earlier, now sadly tousled. Oh, why hadn't she been more careful?

Justine shook her head. She rushed forward to try and unknot the ties of Sandrine's painting apron. 'There is no time, *mademoiselle*. He is coming up here now. Your mother could not stop him.'

'Here?' Sandrine gasped. He truly was eager to see her, be with her! But oh, the room was a mess, a tangle of canvas and paints and rags, and she had quite tumbled apart herself. She ran around, shoving things under chairs, until she heard someone on the stairs outside. She went perfectly still, smiling, trying to stay calm, to be elegant.

She heard the door open and spun around to see Alain standing in the doorway. *Her* doorway. It was stunning, like one of those fantastical dreams dropped into real life. He looked even more impossibly gorgeous, windswept, his eyes glowing. She stared and stared, utterly frozen.

'Do forgive me, Mademoiselle Jaubert,' he said, and raked his hand through his hair. He seemed quite embarrassed at his impetuousness. He wouldn't quite look at her, and she felt a tiny touch of cold doubt. This wasn't quite how she pictured the scene. 'I have come to see if you would care for a drive this afternoon. I am not sure how long this sunshine will last.'

Sandrine swallowed hard, praying she would find

her voice. 'I should like that very much, Monsieur d'Alency,' she squeaked out. 'I fear I am a bit, er, untidy, though.'

Justine slipped out, and Alain glanced at Sandrine, then glanced away again, his study taking in the whole room. She wasn't sure he really saw it, though, he seemed so distant. 'You look most charming, I assure you, *mademoiselle*. Are you quite sure I'm not taking you away from your work? Your mother said it can be hard to pull you away.'

Sandrine laughed. 'Only because she wants someone to sit and admire her embroidery for hours on end. I hardly lock myself in here all the time. It's merely my little art room.'

Something seemed to spark in his eyes, and he moved around, taking in a sketch, a scene, a paintbox. She nudged the wedding-gown sketchbook deeper beneath a cushion. 'You truly are an artist, then?'

'Oh, no, not an *artist*, though I dare say I should like to be one. It's a dear dream, an escape, more than anything.'

'An escape into this room?'

'Yes. My very own little space. Also an escape into my own mind, where no one can see what I'm doing, thinking. Where I am free. The colours and lines, the emotions they create, they take me there. I cannot travel as I would like, so I go in my mind.' Sandrine was astonished; she'd never said such things to anyone, never told anyone her deepest hopes and dreams. What was it about Alain?

He glanced at her, very still and watchful. 'I envy you that. What a marvellous gift it must be. I, too, would like to see new places.'

He sounded so wistful, Sandrine's heart ached for him. 'You have no place where you can escape?'

'Once I did, I think. But life makes demands.' He turned back to the painting he examined, an image of the sea at evening, everything holding its breath as if it waited for something very profound. 'This is quite good. Very good.'

'Do you think so?' Sandrine said, feeling ridiculously pleased by the little compliment. 'I wasn't sure I quite captured that quiet sense I wanted…'

He stepped to the easel where she had just been working, and reached for the canvas cover. 'And what is this one?'

She stepped forward, frantic to stop him looking. 'Oh, no, that one is very rough still! Far from ready for anyone to look at it.'

The cover had already fallen away though, and he took in the sweep of the unfinished lines, the roiling, passionate emotions she was so desperate to let out. 'How extraordinary,' he said quietly. 'Where is this? Cornwall?'

Sandrine bit her lip. 'Yes. I have never been there, but my father says it makes him think of Normandy. I do read a great deal, and I think I can see it all in my mind. A place of such wild drama, such human truth. So many fierce, real emotions. I do so wish I could find a place that reflects all that I feel inside. That accepts it.'

'You have captured that perfectly. I would never have imagined the colours of a sky could show such longing,' he said quietly, and she wondered if he, too, yearned for that freedom and authenticity. If maybe, just maybe, they could look for that together.

'Have you been there? You've probably seen so much more of the world than I have.'

He was still looking at the painting, examining every inch of it. 'It has always been my great hope to travel. To test myself, make my own way.' He said nothing more, studying the painting rather than looking at her.

'I understand.' And she did. She, too, wanted so much more than the little corner of London she was allowed. 'I'm sure one day you will. How have you not…?' She broke off, embarrassed. He had no money for such travel, of course. That was why he was here today. She'd been a fool to forget that for even a moment. 'I think you must suit a place like Cornwall, or Normandy.'

He glanced at her over his shoulder, a bemused little smile on his face. 'How so?'

'You have that freedom inside of you.'

He laughed. 'Do I?'

'Yes. Maybe you should travel to Spain. El Greco is one of my favourite artists. So dramatic and full of expression. You remind me of one of his princes or saints.'

He laughed humourlessly, and she sensed he distanced himself again. 'I am no saint, I promise you, Mademoiselle Jaubert.'

Sandrine knew that must be true, in the worldly sense of the word. She'd heard of his love of cards and horses, probably of women, too. His easy, confident way through the London world. But she knew now that so many other things lurked beneath. If only he would let her see them, let her show him all of herself in return! If only she could bridge that distance between them. 'One needn't be a saint in deed to pose as one. I am sure no one believes the models in his *Madonna and Child with Saint Martina and Saint Agnes* were actually virgins floating above the rest of the world. Imperia Cognati, who was Raphael's favourite model, was a famous courtesan, I think.'

'What a surprise you are, *mademoiselle*.'

She could read nothing in his cool tone; it was quite maddening. 'I told you, I do read a great deal. But don't tell my mother that.' She tilted her head to examine him more closely, that sharp line of his cheekbones, the tumble of his hair, the shadows behind his eyes. 'I really would like to paint you. The light seems to love the angles of your face.'

He shook his head brusquely. 'I'm sure I would prove most unsatisfactory to your vision. Shall we go out before the daylight has faded? I borrowed a carriage, and should hate for it to go to waste.'

Sandrine felt her cheeks heat with embarrassment, at how easily she'd let her guard down with him. She was glad he couldn't see the stacks of her sketchbooks, all those gowns and hats! How silly he would think her. She tugged the cover down over her painting. 'Yes, of course. I'm sorry I kept you so long. Let me just change my frock. I shall only be a moment.'

The day was still quite bright when Sandrine emerged from the house to find Alain waiting with a dashing little curricle, sunny yellow and black. If they couldn't escape London, couldn't fly off on travels, at least they would see it in style that day.

He held out his hand to help her up onto the high seat. She studied it for an instant before she dared take it, resting her fingers on his. That heated spark she remembered when he had touched her before shot through her all over again, like a dash of warm water, a flash of light through a storm, and she shivered. She hated to lose that startling, amazing sensation when she was seated and he let go to climb up beside her.

She sensed the weight of attention on her, eyes watching avidly from the drawing-room windows, as she smoothed the skirts of her smoke-blue dress around her. Her mother, no doubt, watching anxiously, hoping her odd little daughter would do nothing to ruin those aristocratic dreams just as they seemed so close. Alain gathered up the reins, his arm brushing hers before he quickly drew away.

Sandrine smiled up at him from beneath the brim of her bonnet, taking in that beautiful profile she still itched to sketch, the pale glow of his eyes. He slanted a little smile down at her, too quickly gone.

'Thank you for taking me out today,' she said. 'It was all feeling rather—close indoors.'

He guided them smoothly, expertly into traffic. 'I know the feeling. You should try sitting in a drawing room with my two sisters. Ribbons and fashion papers and slippers everywhere. And the shrieking. *Mon Dieu!* One moment they will try and tear each other's hair out, and the next they are laughing and whispering as bosom companions.' He moved around another vehicle, and she couldn't help but admire his elegant, long-fingered hands in their dark gloves, the easy control he had on the horse, on his surroundings. Driving seemed like breathing to him.

'I should like to have had a sister. Or a brother. It gets rather quiet and lonely being the only one.' The one with all the hopes on her. She wondered again if maybe, possibly, she and Alain could be something else together, find a new way.

'It is rather lonely in my parents' house, too, despite—or maybe because of—all the noise,' he said, his tone light but something darker, sharper, lurking underneath. 'I wish I could have my own little painting room, as you do.'

'Do you like to paint, too?'

'Not at all. I can barely draw a creditable square. But the silence must be heavenly. Perhaps I should take up writing poetry, so I could claim a quiet little library somewhere. I wonder if feelings could be caught in words as you do in colours. I should like that.'

'You would no doubt be a famous poet. You are much more handsome than Byron.' And there was that *something*, that something deeper and darker just beneath. Something she wished she could unearth from beneath his cool distance.

He slanted her an amused glance from under the brim of his hat. 'Really? I fear my versifying at present is quite as terrible as my drawing, so looks would be all I had to begin with.'

Sandrine waved this away. 'Words can be taught, felt. You *look* like a poet, that is the important thing to begin with. Throw in a bit of tormented rakishness, a few lines about beauty like the moon and stars, some tragic endings, and all will go well, I think. I am a painter, not a writer.'

He laughed, and those shadows slid away. She loved that lightness she felt in him then, that easy fun. She hadn't realised how much she longed for such moments in her quiet life. But it was quickly gone, as he seemed to withdraw into himself again. She had to find a way to draw him forward once more. 'You are an expert on poetry, *mademoiselle*? Most ladies seem to be, painters or not.'

Sandrine shrugged, and opened her parasol to twirl it around. 'I read a lot of poetry, it's true. I certainly don't like all of it.'

'Perhaps we should establish a salon, like in the old days in France. One for talented painters and terrible poets,' he mused as they turned a corner and headed towards the park. 'Serve good wine and very little food. We would be very popular.'

He joked, but Sandrine thought it sounded perfect. A circle of friends who loved art, lots of conversation and laughter. A future that was all hers, just as she—and Alain—wanted to build it. Surely he cared about her! Surely he understood. Everything looked terribly bright around her. 'And we shall serve ices from Gunter's; that will be the only food.'

'Ices it is! So, where shall we go today? The gates of the park are just ahead.'

Sandrine studied the carriages and pedestrians making their way towards those gates, a crowd in the bright day. She wanted to keep him to herself for just a while. 'Maybe we could go to the Cavendish Gallery? It's not far.'

'A gallery?'

'They are displaying a beautiful Fra Angelico painting, and have a great many new landscapes I would like to see. I can never persuade my mother to let me visit there enough; she finds it dull.'

'I don't think looking at paintings in your company could ever be dull.' He turned the carriage as easily as she would walk in a different direction. 'How often would you visit such museums and galleries, if you could do whatever you liked?'

'Oh, every day, I fear! The curators would get very tired of me indeed. And I would find all the teachers I could, take lessons that offer a bit more in-depth tuition

than my old drawing master could give. Though...'
She hesitated, wondering if she was talking too much, as she seemed to do with him. He was easy company, despite the way his beauty made her fidget and blush. A good listener.

'Though what?' he asked, his tone full of curiosity.

'Well, sometimes when I look at great art, truly great art, I feel terribly overwhelmed. Sad. Adrift.' She couldn't explain it, really, not even to herself, that intense longing that would sometimes come over her.

'How so? I can definitely agree that such feelings could leave us confused.'

'Yes. Have you ever longed for something so very much, craved it deep in your bones, hungered for it?'

He blinked, and suddenly seemed very distant. His gaze turned inward, to something hidden, unseen. 'Yes. I have.'

Sandrine wondered what it was, what made him sad. If only she could soothe it. 'That is what I've often felt about art, true art. And when I see something of such beauty, such transcendence, I fear I could never reach such heights myself. Never touch such sublime, aching perfection. Never say what I really want to say.'

The silence stretched between them for a long moment, and she wondered if she'd babbled too much. Said too much. He gave her such a feeling that she'd done something wrong, when all she wanted was to impress him. 'I am sure you will attain all of that. I may not be an expert on art, but I know what I saw in your work, *mademoiselle*. I know what it made me feel. You must use your gift, bring it to others.'

She feared she might start crying at those simple words, that affirmation she'd never heard from anyone before. She had moved him with her work. It had meant something to someone, even if only for a moment. She turned away, blinking hard.

Luckily, they soon arrived at the gallery, a sombre, pale stone edifice whose blank windows gave no clue to the riches that lay beyond, and she had an excuse to fuss with her parasol, to dash away those tears. Someone came to take the carriage, and Alain helped her to the walkway. She squeezed his hand, grateful beyond anything she could say, excited she could share this place with him. She dashed up the narrow marble steps to the doors, stepping inside to take a deep breath of the deliciously cool air, scented with the faint whiff of oil paint, of old paper, of hushed and awed silence. It was like stepping into a sanctuary, and he was there beside her. She was not alone.

'I wish I could look at everything all at once,' she said, spinning around to all the galleries that stretched from the foyer.

'What about—this one?' Alain said. He started towards the doorway to the left, and Sandrine scurried after him. She found herself in a treasure box, a room of crimson walls lined with the vivid colours, the dramatic lines and palpable emotions of seascapes, ancient battles, gods and goddesses.

'One day, Mademoiselle Jaubert, your work will be

right here,' he said, his tone full of confidence, full of her hopes.

'If I work hard enough, perhaps. But there is the Fra Angelico over there! Come, let me show it to you.' She led him to her favorite scene, a Madonna on a gold-leafed throne, a lily in one hand, her bright head bent tenderly towards the child on her lap, who also held a flower up to her. 'The splendour of the colours are incredible, of course, and the way the light slants and curves to touch her face. But I have always yearned for that sweetness in her eyes as she looks at her child...'

'Yes,' he said softly. 'So tender. You have a fine sensibility, Mademoiselle Jaubert.'

'Alain! Imagine seeing you here. You're the last person I would expect,' a man called out merrily.

Sandrine turned to see a tall gentleman, with sandy brown hair and kind, dark eyes, hurrying towards them. Alain stiffened at her side.

'I did not think you were much of a connoisseur of art,' he said, clapping Alain on the shoulder. He examined Sandrine with an admiring glint in his eyes she wished she could see in Alain's. 'But I dare say you are hiding here to keep this beautiful flower to yourself. Most unfair of you.'

'Louis, this is Mademoiselle Jaubert. And this flattering coxcomb is, I fear, an old schoolfriend of mine, Monsieur Louis Brissac.'

Monsieur Brissac bowed low over Sandrine's hand, making her laugh. 'A fellow citizen of France! No wonder you have such elegance, as only a French lady could.'

'I fear I barely remember France at all,' Sandrine said, delighted to meet someone who knew Alain. 'And I would have thought neither of you gentlemen could be old enough to have attended a French school.'

'Alas, no, but our schoolmaster was from Brittany. A bit of home on our new shores, where I, of course, excelled at languages and mathematics, and Alain excelled at *paress, lazinesse*.'

She laughed even more, picturing the two of them as youngsters dashing through the school corridors, creating havoc. 'Oh, I should like to know so much more, *monsieur*.'

'You do sadly misrepresent me to the young lady, Louis,' Alain chided. Did he actually sound—embarrassed? And was that a *blush* on his cheeks? Sandrine was even more intrigued.

'But if she hears that everyone at school thought you a paragon, as well as the perfection of your cursed face, she would never look at *me*, I fear.' Louis sighed. 'But coincidentally I am here with Monsieur Aurac, our very schoolmaster! He has returned to live in Hampstead, and has tried to turn me from poetry to instill a love of art as well.'

Alain went very still. 'Monsieur Aurac?'

Louis nodded, and shot Alain a long look. 'Yes, and his granddaughter, of course, who has come to keep house for him. I am sure you do remember the lovely Danielle?'

'Well, I should very much like to meet them,' Sandrine said. How wonderful it would be to know more of his past, of what had come to make him the intriguing man he was now! She was overcome with curiosity.

'Yes, you must,' Louis said. He took her arm and led her away towards the gallery door, chatting of old pranks they had once pulled at school. Sandrine glanced back to see Alain frozen in place, watching them go, and she wanted to run back to him, to ask what was suddenly amiss.

'Surely I should escort you home soon, *mademoiselle*,' he called.

'What fustian, Alain!' Louis said with a laugh. 'Monsieur Aurac will be so happy to see you again. You were his favourite pupil.'

Sandrine's head whirled with confusion at how suddenly their lovely day had changed. Alain seemed so distant now. What was happening? Maybe she should go back. But it was too late; they had stepped into another gallery.

A white-haired gentleman in an old-fashioned long, dark coat, leaning heavily on a carved walking stick, was examining a sculpture. Beside him was the most beautiful young lady Sandrine thought she'd ever seen. If she had more skill in portraits or mythological scenes, she would certainly paint her as a statuesque Athena, or a goddess of beauty.

A plain pelisse of dull lavender and a simple straw bonnet edged with just a narrow blue ribbon couldn't disguise the fact that she looked like the Renaissance princesses in the paintings around them. Tall, willowy-slim, she seemed so elegantly remote with a faint smile on rosebud lips, dark eyes large in a fair, heart-shaped face. Gleaming golden waves of hair peeked from under her hat.

Sandrine felt some strange, chilly touch of disquiet as she studied the pair, and she could not fathom why. They seemed entirely ordinary, despite the lady's beauty; they promised information on Alain's past, his character. But she wished she'd taken Alain's hint to depart, and now it was too late. The gentleman glimpsed them, his faded brown eyes widening and a smile touching his lips that made his resemblance to the lady clear.

'Alain! My dearest boy. It has been far too long,' he said, and made a slow path forward to clasp Alain's hand. Alain bowed, but she noticed he did not quite meet the man's eyes, and did not turn towards the lady.

'Monsieur Aurac. It is indeed a pleasure to see you again,' Alain answered. He bowed towards the lady. 'And Mademoiselle Aurac.' She curtseyed, studying the wall over Alain's shoulder.

'It is quite like the bright old days, with you and Louis here with us,' Monsieur Aurac said. 'I would think myself back at Lycée St André again. I hope you still study your Latin.'

'Alain has been terribly lazy, *monsieur*, you would be shocked,' Louis jested. 'He is only for horses and cards these days!'

Monsieur Aurac sadly shook his head. 'Such a

shame. You were always one of my brightest boys. Always reading your Virgil, your Vassari.'

'Only under your sterling influence, *monsieur*,' Alain said. 'I have not time for books now.'

'But he is becoming a connoisseur of art with Mademoiselle Jaubert, I do believe,' Louis said. 'He will be back to his Vasari in no time.' He clapped Alain on the shoulder.

Monsieur Aurac turned to Sandrine, his eyes sharpening with interest. 'Indeed? Well, so would I, if I were fifty years younger. Are you an artist, then, Mademoiselle...?'

'Monsieur Aurac, this is Mademoiselle Sandrine Jaubert,' Alain offered. But Sandrine had the strange sense he would have preferred not to make the introduction, would have rather left right away. Was he ashamed of her, of her family? Yet he had not seemed one for snobbery before this moment. She was deeply puzzled.

'I am pleased to meet you, Mademoiselle Jaubert,' the schoolmaster said.

'And I you, *monsieur*. Monsieur d'Alency and Monsieur Brissac speak of your school so fondly.'

His brown eyes sparkled. 'Ah! Perhaps one day you may like to send your own sons there? The new schoolmaster is different, of course, but still offers fine tutelage. And there is an art master, as well, and tutelage in art history. Any parent who is an artist themselves would appreciate that.'

Danielle Aurac shifted on her feet and glanced away,

and Sandrine fought against that wretched blush rising in her cheeks. 'I—well, art is very important to any education. I fear I am not a *real* artist myself, merely a great appreciator.'

'She is too modest, *monsieur*. Her art is astounding, and Louis is correct that I am seeing it in a new way with her help,' Alain said.

'Then I should like to see it,' Monsieur Aurac said. He suddenly laughed. 'Ah, yes. Jaubert. I think we are to meet you at Alain's mother's dinner next week, *oui*? I shall enjoy seeing more of your work then.'

Sandrine was utterly confused. She glanced at Alain, who looked just as puzzled. 'Dinner, *monsieur*?'

'Yes. We received our invitation just this morning, did we not, Danielle? So fortunate we are in Town just now.'

'Indeed, Grandpère,' the lady said, and her voice was just as lovely as the rest of her, musical, silvery. 'You must not tire yourself before then. We should return to our lodgings for now.'

'Perhaps, perhaps,' Monsieur Aurac murmured. 'Ah, I have been most impolite! Mademoiselle Jaubert, you must meet my granddaughter, Danielle Aurac. She has been my angel, looking after me so very well. Indulging my wild whims to see galleries and museums and libraries all the time when we are in the centre of Town.'

'She has always been an angel,' Louis cried, clasping his hand to his heart. 'Always soothing the hearts of wild schoolboys with her kindness and serenity.'

Danielle laughed softly. 'And you have always been much too kind, Louis. How do you do, Mademoiselle Jaubert? It is always pleasant to meet a friend of Alain's. He was long a favourite pupil of my grandfather.'

'So you grew up at the school, too, *mademoiselle*?' Sandrine asked. Alain was very quiet, very still, yet there was something in the air around him, something taut and tense. Was this why he seemed so reserved with her? His dreams were elsewhere?

'Indeed. My parents sadly perished in France, and Grandpère always took wonderful care of me. I had lessons along with the pupils, as well as music and dance, and made such fine friends.'

Well-educated and cultured, as well as goddess-beautiful. Sandrine sighed, and felt as tiny and pale as a wren. She wished she could hide, shrink down and be invisible. Had she been so very foolish to think Alain could ever admire her?

But she could not run. They chatted for a bit longer of things such as the school now, and the Auracs' retirement in Hampstead, until Monsieur Aurac said, 'Perhaps you are correct, *chère* Danielle, I should seek my rest. Maybe you would walk with us, Mademoiselle Jaubert? I should enjoy hearing your artistic opinion on those landscapes over there.' She took the older gentleman's arm, and walked with him towards the wall of Titians that waited, happy to chat about their colours and strength. But she was all too aware that Alain and the beautiful Danielle had slipped out of the gallery, and she did not see them until it was time to leave once more. The uncertainty felt so cold, when earlier in the afternoon she'd been so very happy.

As the Auracs found a hansom, Alain helped Sandrine up into their carriage and they turned from the gallery back into the bustle and life of the street. The quiet between them stretched out for long moments, as Alain seemed deep in his thoughts and Sandrine felt vaguely unsure of what had happened. What *would* happen.

'The Auracs seem very kind,' she ventured into the silence. 'Studying at his school must have been interesting.'

'Yes. I was very fortunate to end up there at Lycée St André, not a harsh English sort of place with cold-water baths and non-stop cricket,' he answered distantly.

'Do you still see them often?'

'Not very. Not since Monsieur Aurac retired, and my duties to my parents have started to keep me busier.'

'And his granddaughter keeps house for him?' The beautiful Danielle. Sandrine wished she wouldn't feel such a jealous pang thinking about her.

He paused. 'Yes.'

Sandrine turned her head to study the shops as they got near the park. A long, distant moment of silence passed, until Alain said quietly, 'I am sure my parents are looking forward to having you and your family for the dinner party at their home soon. You should feel honoured—they rarely entertain at all!'

'Maybe it's for a—special occasion?' she ventured, remembering how her father said Alain would soon be proposing. She'd been overjoyed to think about that before; now she was not quite so sure. It was all very swift, and she didn't know how to bridge that distance she sensed between them.

Alain drew the carriage into the entrance to the park and moved them to a crawl as he spoke to her. 'Mademoiselle Jaubert—Sandrine. I fear my parents may have rather got ahead of themselves, but I'm sure it's only because of their—enthusiasm.'

She shook her head, confused. 'Enthusiasm? For dinner parties?'

He smiled at her gently. 'I know we haven't known each other very long. But I think we must both be aware of our parents' hopes.'

'I...' A small flutter, of something like excitement, nervousness, uncertainty, hope, all jumbled together, made breathing suddenly difficult. Was it happening now? Was she reacting correctly? She didn't quite know what to do. Surely he had to like her more than she sensed. 'I have an idea, yes. My mother often despairingly mentions how soon my birthday is approaching. I'm sure she thinks I shall collapse into a withered old crone as soon as the clock strikes, and then I'll never be out from under their feet.'

He laughed, and something seemed to relax inside of him. He drew the carriage to a standstill in a small turn in the path, and turned towards her. When his gray eyes were on her, she felt steadier. If only they were in this together, she could find a way to move forward. Could be more sure of herself. 'You could never be any sort of *crone*. My parents also seem sure I am wasting my life, that I need a steady influence, a path.'

Not to mention money, Sandrine thought with a tinge of disquiet, just as her parents longed for a fine French title. Together they might be, but not equal. Not free. 'Our parents seem to have much in common.'

'I always knew of their expectations, Sandrine, just as I'm sure you have. So much was lost for them in France. We owe them so much.' He suddenly reached for her hand, his touch warm through their gloves, strong and reassuring. 'But I never expected you.'

'Me?'

'Yes. You are so thoughtful, Sandrine, you see the world in such colour and beauty. You understand people, too, in a way most of us cannot. You're very special.'

She was *special*. Sandrine had to fight the urge to hug herself, to laugh wildly and spin around. No one had ever thought she was special before, and that he of all people did—it was astounding. Marvellous. 'As are you! I've never met anyone like you, either. And I love how you see that art is so important to me, not just as something to pass the time, but something…'

'Something you *are*.'

'Yes!'

'Then I know you see, as I do, how we can help each other. Find some freedom together. Life may not be arranged just as we would wish, but I'm sure we can build something fine together.'

That hope, that delicate, beautiful hope, flowered and bloomed. 'I wasn't expecting you, either. I'm very sure you're right. We can find an understanding between us.'

'Then, would you do me the great honour of giving me your hand in marriage?' he said, squeezing her hand, his smile widening until it seemed to encompass the whole world. 'It would give my parents something to announce at their dinner!'

Sandrine laughed, giddy with joy. How had her life come together so gloriously, so suddenly? 'Yes! Yes, of course I will.'

He leaned down and kissed her cheek, his warm lips caressing her skin for an instant, leaving tingling delight behind. Her doubts vanished, and everything around her seemed just right. He might seem distant now, but that would surely end very soon. Things would turn out right. They had to.

Chapter Four

Alain studied himself in the looking glass as he tried to tie his cravat fashionably, to make himself look presentable and respectable for his fiancée's family. His *fiancée*. His betrothed.

His fingers fumbled on the crisp muslin, and he resisted the urge to run his fingers through his hair, to muss the carefully tamed curls Catherine and Françoise had worked so hard on. They'd told him he had to look his very best tonight.

None of this felt real. He'd longed to prove himself in the world, to make his way, until time ran out for those ambitions. That felt even more dreamlike than anything else, that a lady might actually wish to marry him. Especially a lady like Sandrine.

His hands went still as he thought of her, of her sweet smiles, her soft curls and gentle manners. The sparkle in her bright green eyes as she shared art with him, shared a new way of looking at the world. She'd entirely surprised him. He'd expected her to be haughty, and she was kind. Snobby, and she took in every bit of the world around her. She'd seemed so quiet when he first glimpsed her at Madame de Fleurieu's, so shy. And it was true she didn't chatter, didn't preen, but she was funny. Observant. Pretty. She was moved by beauty, created beauty, had such depth. She was interested in people, and they felt comfortable around her once they sensed that interest. It was amazing.

He'd known one day he would have to marry, and despite any desperate hopes for fortune's reversal, his marriage could not be to Danielle. Now he had to face facts, face his duty, find a lady willing to make that bargain. He hadn't expected it would be to someone he could really like. That heated burst of lightning when he touched her hand—so entirely unexpected. She certainly *was* pretty, no denying it, her beauty growing the more one knew her, talked to her. When she laughed, those green eyes shimmered like a summer's day.

He closed his eyes, and remembered how she had looked when she studied the Fra Angelico painting. So absorbed, so enthralled. He'd felt sure in that moment that maybe he could find something to offer her after all. He could give her that sort of freedom. Surely she was bound just as he was in family duty. If they were married, she would have the protection to pursue her art, to travel and see museums and galleries, take lessons, seek the recognition she was due.

He opened his eyes, and found he had mangled the cravat beyond saving. He tossed it aside and reached for another. He had to stay on the path now, remember his duty, what he could give Sandrine, not be distracted. Not be selfish, as he'd always been. Not make things more complicated than they needed to be.

He had no plans, just hopes. Desperate, desperate hopes.

Sandrine feared she had no idea what to do next. It was her wedding night! Yet the wedding itself had not felt as she imagined; Alain seemed distracted, distant. She had no idea what to do now. Her mother had carefully gone over every detail of the day itself, but when it came to the night, she'd just stammered a few words like, 'Just lie still,' and 'Soon be over,' and left Sandrine in a greater whirl of confusion than before.

She paced the length of the chamber they'd been given for the night, the very grandest guest room in her parents' house, a space she was sure they'd designed just in case the French king in exile ever happened to visit. It was seldom touched, and Sandrine had barely been in it before then.

She studied herself in the dressing-table mirror, smoothing the fall of her loosened hair, comparing it to Danielle Aurac's beautiful golden waves. She knew she couldn't compare, but surely she looked presentable? Attractive, even? She felt so nervous at the thought, the hope, that Alain would think so.

She sat down on the edge of the massive bed, smoothing the green brocade counterpane under her palms. Should she pretend to be asleep? Pretend to be eager? She touched the loose fall of her hair, and wondered if she should braid it. Would it look childish? Danielle Aurac was so elegant, with her smooth, golden hair, her oval face that surely never felt a burning blush.

She closed her eyes, and thought again of her mother's embarrassed, whispered words about the night ahead. The vague warnings, the promises it would be over quickly and soon there would be beautiful babies. She wasn't completely foolish; she'd heard whispers among the maids, and knew the logistics of what happened. It didn't sound pleasant.

Yet, whenever Alain touched her, it wasn't frightening at all. Surely there was something there to build on?

If only she knew what it would be like, the marriage bed. That uncertainty made her long to leap out of her skin, to run and scream. She jumped up and dashed to the window, pushing aside the heavy satin draperies to peer out. It had rained for a time after the party, and the street gleamed and glittered in the moonlight. She'd never seen it so bright! Everything looked different with Alain. There was so much out there to explore and discover.

There was a soft knock at the door, and she jumped, nearly knocking over a small table that held a carafe of wine. 'E-enter,' she croaked, wishing she had something more enticing to say.

Alain stepped into the room, and hesitated on the threshold for a moment, almost as if he was shy. But that couldn't be! Alain—unsure? She felt no one who looked like him, a red dressing gown draped over his broad shoulders, his hair curling over his brow in a tumble she longed to smooth back, could possibly be unsure. Yet his hesitant smile made her want to run to him, to wrap him in her arms. She wasn't alone in this.

She straightened the table, feeling silly for doubting. They watched each other, the quiet moving and swirling between them. Oh, how she wished she knew what was expected of her! What he wanted of her. Should she take off her clothes, blow out the candles? Wait for him under the turned-back bedclothes?

She peeked up at him, and found him studying her carefully, his eyes hooded, and very dark. She could read nothing there.

Finally, finally, he took a step towards her and held out his hand. 'Sandrine. Please don't be afraid. I would never hurt you.'

She wasn't so sure of that. Oh, she knew very well he would never, ever hurt her physically. He had nothing of that cruel streak she sensed in some other men, that pleasure in wounding. But her heart—she did fear for that. She couldn't resist going to him, taking his hand. It felt cold under her touch.

'I—don't know what to do,' she admitted.

'Sandrine. You just have to *be*. It's only you and me here tonight.' His arms slid around her waist and drew her closer, slowly, gently, his eyes watching her so carefully as if for any sign she might flee. She couldn't stop shaking, so much longing flowing through her she was sure she would burst with it.

His head bent down towards hers, and his lips touched hers ever so softly. She knew her mother told her not to resist, to just go along with whatever happened, but that was not at all what she wanted to do. What she felt. Every place he touched left tiny droplets of fire behind, and she wanted more. More of what she'd felt when he kissed her before. She eased his dressing gown back from his shoulders, letting her touch slide over the warm silk of his skin, feeling him, knowing him, letting her hunger burst free.

He seemed to feel it, too, for he groaned against her lips, and pulled her closer. They tumbled backwards to the bed, the kiss sliding down into frantic need. Her own dressing gown melted away under his touch, and they were pressed together.

He kissed the corner of her trembling mouth, the curve of her jaw, finding one tiny, sensitive spot. His teeth nipped lightly at that curve behind her ear, and a shudder shot through her body. She ran her fingers along the groove of his back, wondering that she could touch him like that, feel him with her. He was right, it was only them that night. She had no need to be afraid.

Her arms wound around his shoulders, holding him against her as they sank deeper into the feather mattress. He kissed the swell of her breast above the lace edge of her nightdress, caressed her, shockingly tracing the pink of her nipple through the thin silk of her gown. His touch was light, gentle, but it was shocking, glorious.

'Alain,' she gasped, and he gave her what she hoped for, closing his mouth around her aching nipple, rolling his tongue over it.

She moaned, and her hands fell away to twist into the sheets. He lowered himself over her, and she loved how heavy he felt, how small she was with him.

He took one of her hands, and pressed it flat to his chest. She felt the roughness of hair under her palm, that heat of his skin, the pounding of his heart that echoed her own. 'Oh, Sandrine. I want to make you happy, to give you such pleasure. Always.'

'I want that, too,' she whispered. 'Pleasure for us. So much. I just—I've never...'

'Trust me, *chérie*. I beg you, just trust me.'

She nodded. 'Always.' He kissed her again. He tasted her deeply, and when she melted into him, relishing the delight of that moment, he gently slid her gossamer-thin gown over her shoulders, skimmed it along her body, watching every inch he bared with such hunger in his eyes, until he tossed it to the floor.

His fingertips caressed her shoulders, the soft curve of her breasts, the curve of her waist, gentle, enticing. She shivered, adrift on a warm sea of pure sensation. All fear was gone, all uncertainty. This was where they were meant to be.

He lowered himself between her trembling thighs, nudging them apart, and dared to touch the very core of her with the tips of his fingers. Lightly, skilfully. She gasped at the sparkling sensations that shot through her, and couldn't stop wriggling beneath him. He wouldn't let her go so easily. She grabbed his hand as she sensed it would move even deeper. 'Are you *sure* you're supposed to do that?'

He laughed, the sound so wonderful. 'Sandrine. My betrothed. I do wish you wouldn't *think* so much. Not just at this moment. Please, please, let me just help you *feel*.' That touch slid back over her. 'Can you trust me?'

She stared up at him as he rose on his knees above her, and she loved his face, so handsome, so tender, so shaded in light and dark. So intent only on her. She cast aside that last shred of doubt. She had to trust him. Her heart was his.

She nodded slowly, and he smiled down at her. He took her hand, where her new rings sparkled, and pressed it again to his heart, where she could feel the powerful rhythm of it moving in time with hers. It was impossible to breathe, they were bonded so closely in that moment.

'I want to give you pleasure, Sandrine, to make you happy if I can,' he said.

She stared up at him. Did he not know how happy she already was, how she was sure she would float up into the sky and lose herself completely in the giddy happiness of that moment? She'd thought this would never be her life, never be such a dream come true. 'Yes.'

He swooped down and covered her mouth with his, kissing her with all the pent-up hunger that had been growing between them ever since they had met. Their kiss was all-consuming, humid, hot, banishing all else.

He touched her most secret place again, combing his fingertips through the damp curls before easing inside her, shockingly, wonderfully, stoking her desire to new, bonfire heights.

A strange little mewing sound she didn't recognise escaped before she could catch it as he found that one perfect little spot. His thumb caressed it, harder, faster, and she cried out.

'I'm so sorry, Sandrine,' he whispered.

'Sorry?' she murmured, confused.

'I can't wait any longer.'

She nodded. 'I'm ready.' Oh, so ready.

She closed her eyes, determined to remember every second, absorb every sensation. He slid carefully, slowly into her, his every muscle tense as if he was trying to be perfectly careful of her. He braced his arms to either side of her, his muscles corded, holding himself above her. When she eased her palms down his back, she felt the dampness of his exertions, the taut strength of him, his sheathed desire that echoed her own. She longed for it to fly free!

At last, at last, he plunged forward and they were joined as one. She held him close, tracing the groove of his lean backside, the length of his spine, with her fingertips, that power of him as he shifted and moaned and surged. She felt a twinge of sharp pain, a stretching, burning sensation, but then only the soft, spreading heat of pleasure. She raised her hips to draw him in even deeper.

He braced his forearms to either side of her head and held himself very still for a moment. His face was tense, his eyes closed.

'Please,' she whispered.

Slowly, enticingly, he eased back and rocked forward again, moving a little faster. With each movement they were joined more deeply, and she learned to move with him. A delicious, tingling glow spread through her body, to the very tips of her toes, and she gasped with the joy of it.

She wrapped her legs around his lean hips as he thrust into her, faster and faster.

'Alain!' she cried. 'I can't—I'm...'

'Just let it happen. Be free, Sandrine!'

So she did. She let go of everything else, burst into a fiery explosion of joy.

'Sandrine!' he shouted. His body arched above hers, his back bowed. 'Sandrine.'

He fell to the bed beside her, their limbs entwined as the sparkling sunbursts faded into cool, beautiful shadows. She felt the heat of his breath against her shoulder, as ragged as her own. His arm wrapped around her waist, holding her close, and she lazily reached up to twine her shaking fingers in the damp, silken strands of his hair.

How very weak and tired she felt! Yet also how light and, and yes, free. Why had she ever been scared of this act, this moment? It was perfection.

His breath slowed as he slid down into sleep, and she sat up to press a kiss to his damp brow. He sighed, and his clasp tightened on her, wanting to be so near even in exhausted sleep. Married life would surely not be bad at all.

Chapter Five

Alain slowly opened his eyes to find the light of a new day washing over him from the half-open draperies. That light, pinkish-gold, seemed to change everything after the tumult and unexpected magic of the night before. He rolled over to find Sandrine, but she wasn't there. A bit of paper on her pillow said, 'Went to sketch. Good morning, my husband!'

He smiled to see that scrawled note. Husband. He remembered every wondrous moment, the silken feel of her skin under his touch, the little moans she had made, the tumble of her hair over his arm. He remembered *everything*. He'd never thought his wedding night could be so—so perfect. So filled with heat and light. That it could change everything in only a few moments.

His world was shaken up, turned inside out, made bright and magical.

He slowly sat up amid the wrinkled sheets, shaking back the tangle of curls from his brow. Sandrine was nowhere to be seen, but her rosy perfume lingered in the air, in the bedclothes heaped around him. He stretched his delightfully aching limbs and smiled.

Maybe he was just over-dramatising matters. It was good, yes, pleasurable. *Very*. But deep down, he knew something enormous had happened. He hadn't expected to desire Sandrine so much; he hadn't even planned to make love to her, only to talk to her, tell her his plans, tell her the truth. But one look, one touch, and he was lost.

He did have to tell her, his wife, about his past. About Danielle, about his confusion. She deserved that. She deserved to know that he would always help her, would make sure she could pursue her art, pursue whatever she wanted from life. He longed to tell her everything. She was the most understanding person he'd ever met, the best listener. He...

He *liked* her. As well as desiring her, he liked her, he wanted to hear her thoughts, valued her advice. Most extraordinary.

He clambered out of bed and quickly dressed in breeches and loose shirt, trying to smooth his tangled hair. There was a knock at the door, a discreet little cough.

'Yes, what is it?' he called impatiently.

'I am very sorry indeed, *monsieur*, to wake you at this—sort of moment,' the butler called. 'But there is a caller. She says it is most urgent indeed. She is in the small sitting room.'

A caller? Curious, fearful something might have happened to one of his sisters and it was an emergency, he answered, 'I shall be there in a moment.' He hastily donned the rest of his clothes, and hurried downstairs, hoping it could be taken care of before Sandrine returned from her sketching.

To his shock, it was Danielle who waited for him there. Danielle, pacing the length of the room, her hands twisted together.

'Danielle?' he said, closing the door behind him. A tangle of emotions flooded through him: fear, curiosity, hope. Mostly a strange sense that she suddenly belonged to the past, that she should not be here in the present, the future. 'What is amiss? Is it your grandfather?'

'*Non*, nothing like that,' she cried. She rushed to him, reached for his hand, but he slid away from her. 'I had to see you, *mon cher*. After your wedding, seeing what was really happening...'

'Happening?' he said.

'You marrying. Moving on in your life—without me.'

Alain was baffled. He studied her carefully, saw the gleam of desperation in her eyes, the tight line of her lips. What could have happened? Their lives had long been set, and any hope they might have had was gone. He found he could not even mourn it now. 'You, too, are betrothed. To Lord Darby.'

'Because I must be! How else can I live? But I thought of something last night. A plan.'

'Plan?'

'How we can be together! Our spouses surely have interests they want to pursue in life. Why should not we? Why can we not be together in secret? It would hurt no one!'

Alain felt a cold wave of shame that he, too, had considered just such a thing. But he knew now, after the night with Sandrine, that could not be. Life was different now. It had to be. But he still felt tenderness for Danielle, for what he'd felt for her, what they'd been to one another. He took her hands between his.

'We must move ahead with our lives, Danielle, you know we must,' he said gently. 'You will always be my friend…'

'Friend?' she cried. She suddenly went up on her tiptoes and flung her arms around his neck, holding so tightly he could not let go, move away. Her lips pressed to his, warm, soft, caressing, seeking. For an instant, a mere flash, he felt himself respond, felt himself reach for her. Until he remembered Sandrine—and reached up to gently unwind her arms.

'I love you,' she said. 'And I know you love me, you always have. We can still be together…'

And that was when he heard it. The soft opening of a door, a gasp, and running footsteps. The ruin of something before it could even begin.

An Hour Earlier

Sandrine couldn't stand still for a moment longer. She slipped from the warmth of her bed, the glorious beauty of her sleeping husband, and tiptoed into the sitting room next door, where their luggage waited to travel with them on their honeymoon, her fingers itching for her drawing pencils. She stretched up to push back the window curtains, revelling in the unaccustomed soreness in her legs and arms, so delicious. She let in the rosy, warm early morning light, letting its promise wash over her as that wonderful new day began. Her first day as a married woman! She felt silly for doubting things at all.

She smiled to think of it, to think of the man she'd left sleeping in her bed. *Their* bed. Before, she'd been so nervous about what might happen in those 'marital duties' her mother had whispered about. She'd known the technical process of what happened, and it seemed so very odd. Improbable. But no one said how fun it was! How good it felt, after that first tiny sharpness. How delicious it was. How right.

Or maybe she'd been fortunate. She'd found herself an exceptional husband.

And indeed he was. She hugged herself and twirled around in sheer delight, thinking of how beautiful he was, how powerful, how gentle as he guided her into pleasure. His face as he lost himself in what was happening between them, the rough sound of his whispers.

When she'd woken so early, just as the sky was turning pale grey at the edges and the stars blinked and faded, she knew she wouldn't go back to sleep. She couldn't wake him, as he slept so peacefully beside her, her ancient god looking so young in his dreams. The house was still quiet, the perfect time for a bit of drawing.

Her sketchbooks were packed in one of the many

valises and trunks ready to leave that day. She turned from the sunrise and dug around for her precious papers and pencils.

When she found them, she turned to the sketches she'd begun of Alain. How hard she'd worked to capture the essence of him, the elusive self he hid behind his charming smiles and careless manners. How she longed to capture every, every detail! The way his hair curled just so at his temple, the arc of his jaw. Now she considered all the new details she'd discovered while she studied him in his slumber. The softness of his lower lip, the line of his cheekbone, the shadows where his beard was growing at his jaw.

The little frown that came and went as he dreamed, the power of his bare shoulder against the embroidered edge of the sheet. How beautiful it all was. How enticing. And she would have years and years of life as his wife to study every bit of him.

She flipped to a new page and started a new image, one just for her, of her husband asleep.

Some time later the pencil suddenly broke off at the tip, and she muttered as she saw it was the last in that packet. She reached for another bag, hoping the fresh supplies she'd bought at the art supply shop were there, but then she remembered she'd left the bag in the library downstairs. She quickly found her slippers, and slipped out of the room and down the stairs.

The house was not as empty and silent as she'd hoped. Voices, low, intense, echoed from the library. Something cold and hard formed in the pit of her stomach, and she knew, *knew*, she should turn away. Yet she could not. Some force carried her forward.

She eased the door open a crack, and saw Alain with Danielle Aurac, their arms around each other. 'I know you love me, you always have,' Danielle said. 'We can still be together!'

Sandrine slowly shut the door and backed away. *Fool, fool*, she told herself. She should have known that all this was too good to be real, to be anything but a dream. She ran back upstairs. So warm only moments before, so aglow with possibility, with hope, suddenly she was sure she was turning to ice. Her skin, her fingers, her mind, all frozen in place.

She was just a fool. She'd thought herself so lucky, her future so bright and hopeful, and all the while the man she'd thought she was falling in love with, the man she was to share her life with, loved another. Loved a beautiful, confident, elegant woman he was kept from by duty. She, Sandrine, was the duty, and she was helpless to change it, helpless to steer her own life. What could she do now?

If only she could go back to the moment she'd woken up next to Alain, so happy, so hopeful. If only she could go back to before the sunrise, to stay in bed beside Alain, to be who she was then.

But she knew she couldn't wish that now. It was always better to know what was real than to live in cloudy dreams.

She turned to a fresh page in her sketchbook, and started to draw something, anything. A meadow, the sky. She wanted to lose herself in her own created world, as she had so often, but it was elusive now.

The door to the sitting room suddenly opened, before she could pretend to be ignorant, to be a blithe bride. Startled, she glanced over her shoulder to see Alain standing there. How beautiful he looked, his tousled hair, his wrinkled shirt, hastily donned and speaking of intimacies. Sandrine might have hoped her girlish longing for him, for all he seemed to stand for in his confidence and carelessness and brightness, would have frozen along with her heart. Yet it was still there, so strong, reaching out for him in such yearning. She turned back to her sketchbook still open on the table, blinking back warm tears she would give anything for him not to see.

Alain frowned. 'Sandrine, please…' he began. Then his glance fell to the little package on the carpet, the portrait peeking out from the edge of the note. His face shifted, changed, grew serious, and she knew it was true. 'What you just saw, it was nothing. I don't know why Danielle would come here now. Oh, my dear Sandrine. I am so sorry…' He broke off, running one shaking hand through his hair, and any wild hope she'd had that she had misunderstood what she'd seen was severed.

Tell her what? Of his love for another woman, maybe that he was going to run away with her? To her horror, she felt a touch of moisture on her cheek as she stared back at him across the vast chasm of the little room and angrily swiped those hateful tears away. She could not lose what little dignity she had left on top of everything else!

'You were going to tell me that you *had* to marry me, I take it?' she managed to whisper. 'I know that. Or, I should have known that. My parents would also not have let me say no. Our families need each other, and we're their most useful tool to get what they desire.'

'It isn't like that at all, Sandrine!' he said, his voice filled with tension. He sat down beside her, and the heat of him, that lemony scent that she loved so much, seemed to mock her. He reached for her hand, but his touch dropped when she flinched. 'That is, maybe it was like that at first. Our families do need each other, and I must do my best for them, for my sisters. But then...'

He was fumbling, not at all like the confident Alain she'd come to know, and she softened towards him. After all, this was a situation neither of them could control. 'Then?'

'Then I came to know you. Your sweetness and kindness.' He gestured at the sketchbook on her lap. 'Your love of art. I know it is not just something you do, not some pleasant past-time, but who you *are*. I know you deserve to pursue it with your whole self.'

Sandrine sniffled. He was not wrong. Art was as necessary to her as sunlight, but no one had seen that until him. Why, why did it all have to go so wrong? 'So you thought I might traipse off to paint and, what, leave you to your love? To you doing what you want in life, making your own way?'

She knew instantly by the look on his face, the flushed chagrin, she'd come close to the mark.

'Not like that,' he said. 'I hoped we could be real friends, could help each other find our happiness. Help each other become ourselves.'

'And now?'

'Danielle is to marry someone else,' he said quietly, tightly. She heard the pain behind those words; he was hurting, too. Sandrine saw they were both trapped.

'I am sorry,' she whispered.

He glanced up at her, a hopeful smile touching the corner of his lips. 'But after last night—surely you see how things have changed? We understand each other fully now, can build a life that suits only us. You know everything about me.'

'But what can suit us? How do you envision the future for us?' Maybe he still envisioned a future with Danielle, with his wife to cover for him. She could never bear that. She would crack under the pain of it all.

He ran his hand through his hair again, leaving it adorably on end, so full of confusion. Sandrine saw then how young he really was, how young they both were, caught in a situation not of their making. 'I'm not sure, Sandrine. We can decide together. We have our freedom now! We have each other. Are we not friends?'

Friends. Of course he did not say they loved each other. That he loved her. He was done with lies now.

She had to be, too, even to herself. She carefully rose to her feet, feeling so stiff and unsteady, so old. She went to the window and stared outside for a long, silent moment. The day was bright now, and it made her ache. That day she'd so longed for, longed to see what it held, now just shone its light on how silly she'd been.

'Freedom. Yes. I think I might wish to find that now.'

'In what way?' he asked, his voice puzzled. She was very glad he didn't come to her side, didn't touch her now. She needed to think clearly.

'I'm not sure,' she said, and she really was not. Not at all. But she knew staying near him, in a marriage she knew was empty, a mere friendship where he thought she was 'sweet and kind' and she longed for all of him, would tear her apart. 'I must go.'

He did come to her side then. She sensed his hand, raised as if to reach for her, then fall to his side. She still wanted to lean on him, feel his arms around her, find that haven she thought she'd discovered in him, but it was all gone.

'Go where?' he asked roughly. 'To Brighton for our honeymoon?'

'Maybe for now.' She realised the house would be awake very soon, that everyone would expect her to take breakfast with them, to laugh and smile as if she hadn't a care in the world. They would be watching her so closely to see how she had fared last night. How could she bear it? 'I don't want to hurt our families, though they are the ones who brought us to this. I don't want them to know. I will leave with you today, and once we reach Brighton, I will decide where I must go next. On my own.'

'Alone? Sandrine, no! What can you mean?' he said, his voice hoarse, full of disbelief, concern. Concern for her, or for himself?

She looked at him at last, into those beautiful eyes that spoke now of shock. 'I mean that I will find a place to stay, to live. You needn't worry, Alain. I shall do nothing to endanger our marriage agreement; your parents and dear sisters will be secure, and my parents will have the connections they want. They won't question me very closely about where I'm actually living, not when they have the society they desire to move in. You can find a way to be close to Mademoiselle Aurac.'

'No, no. I told you, she is marrying another. And now I can see that...' He broke off, shook his head.

'Then you can find someone else to love that way.' She gently touched his hand, trying to reassure him, reassure them both, that something could be salvaged from this. As he'd said, they had their freedom now. 'It will all be for the best.'

He turned his hand, seized her fingers in his, held on tight. If she'd had the wild hope that had filled her that morning, such a touch might have given her happiness once more. But she knew better now. She didn't dare trust. 'The best? But we are married.'

'But we don't have to be. Not in a real way.'

'A real way. What happened last night...' His voice cracked, and he faltered.

Sandrine shook her head, desperate not to remember last night, not to remember the joy of his touch, his kiss. The way it had felt to be joined as one, move as one. 'You'd had too much champagne. We were caught up in the wedding. I do understand.' She didn't, not really. She'd been caught up only in him. But he could never know that.

'That was not it at all! You are so beautiful, Sandrine, so...'

'Don't say *sweet*,' she snapped. She didn't want to be his sweet, understanding little wife. She'd wanted to be his goddess, his true love. How ridiculous she'd been.

She could not look at him a moment longer, not see the confusion in his eyes, the way his jaw grew taut, his lips tighten. She spun away, welcoming the interruption as a knock sounded on the door and a maidservant bustled in. Sandrine could not pretend a moment longer. She rushed into the bedroom, leaving her husband staring after her amid the wreckage.

Chapter Six

Bath, Five years later

'I vow, Sandrine, your gowns make me feel like an empress! Like I have the power to do anything at all,' Mary Campbell declared as she twirled in front of the full-length, gilt-framed mirror of Sandrine's fitting room. The blossom-pink of her new satin gown, with its cream net overdress embroidered with tiny seed pearls into wheat ears and leaves, set off her blonde beauty perfectly.

Sandrine laughed. She wanted to twirl, too, in a burst of satisfaction at her latest creation. It was a fairly new, very fashionable style, and she hadn't been at all sure it would work with her new pattern. But Mary looked lovely, like a golden goddess. Mary had been such a good friend, Sandrine never wanted to disappoint her. 'That is all I want. To make gowns that fill ladies with confidence in their own beauty when they wear them.'

It was the reason she'd opened her business in the first place, to help women find their inner strength as she'd once longed to find hers. She could not help them as she'd like in the outside world, the world of marriage and men, but maybe she could help them find that strength inside. Find belief in themselves through looking and thus feeling their very best. Through fashion that brought out the 'empress' in them all.

She never wanted anyone else to feel as she once had. So small, so foolish, so helpless. Her trust in herself so shattered. Once, she'd only wanted to curl up into a tiny, tight ball and vanish.

In helping other women, she'd found something unexpected—she'd found herself. The Sandrine buried so deep she'd never even glimpsed her before. She relied only on herself now. She would never give a man such power over her spirit again.

A gown was a small enough thing, but silk and lace could be a powerful armour. A way of proclaiming 'This is who I am. This is what I deserve. This is what I desire.'

Not that Mary St Aubin Campbell required much armour. Sandrine studied her friend again, adjusted the drape of the ruffle-edged sleeve, the length of the embroidered hem. Mary, like Sandrine herself, ran her own business, the St Aubin and Briggs Confidential Agency, which made matches for those who desired more than convenience in their marriages, more than an arrangement. Mary was very good at it. She and her sister, Ella, now Countess of Fleetwood, had built up a vast network of clients, a large file of happy marriages. The St Aubin sisters were two of Sandrine's best customers.

Sandrine had even recently created Mary's wedding gown, for her marriage to the impossibly handsome Charles Campbell at St John the Evangelist Church there in Bath. It was a triumph, if Sandrine did say so herself, a confection of shimmering beads and ethereal clouds of net. Like all of her designs, it reflected the lady who wore it rather than disguising her behind whatever was fashionable whether it suited her or not. The design showed Mary's glowing, angelic golden beauty, her love of laughter and fun and romance. Sandrine had spent hours and hours perfecting the embroidery and beading herself.

Yet even the most glorious, iridescent satin could not outshine the love that had emanated from Mary on that sunny winter day, the answering adoration on the face of her bridegroom as she had floated towards him down the aisle. Their passionate romance had filled the whole of the ancient church, expanded like a shimmering bubble that could envelop the whole town, the whole world, in true love.

It had made Sandrine ache to see it, to remember what she had once hoped for and that which had been shattered at her feet before the bridal bouquet even faded. She was ecstatic for her friend, and bursting with pride at all the compliments for the gown. She seldom allowed herself to look back; she had too much to worry about in the now, too much work to do. But in that moment, she'd longed to sob.

She'd shaken those tears away, as she always did, and returned to her shop. It was all she could do now. Alain was gone from her life, and had been for nearly five years.

And now Mary was back from some time at her husband's Scottish castle, ready to reopen her agency and launch Charles's ward, Adele, on her London Season in the spring. Which would naturally require a large order from Sandrine's shop.

Wedding gowns had become something of a speciality for Sandrine, quite against her will, as once she had never wanted to look at another bridal dress again. But word had spread after she had designed a duchess's gown a few years ago, going far beyond even Bath. Everyone had whispered that having an especially beautiful Madame gown on that pivotal day would bring luck, happiness, confidence. Wedding gowns also brought orders for trousseaux, and put wages in the pockets of seamstresses and salesladies. A Madame gown spelled good fortune for so many.

Sandrine didn't often do fittings herself any more, as she'd been able to hire such an accomplished, polished team, and she was kept so busy with designing, running accounts, ordering fabrics. Mary, though, was a dear friend, and Sandrine always enjoyed time laughing and chatting with her.

Not that she was able to have the deepest, most intimate of friendships. Not with the secrets she carried, would always carry. The things she could never say to anyone, could only think about when she was all alone in the darkest part of the night.

She adjusted the ribbon edge of the sleeve. 'There! What do you think? How does that feel?'

Mary circled her arm, giving the regal wave worthy of a true empress. 'It's perfect, of course.'

'Wonderful! I can have it ready on Tuesday, if that suits. The new lavender spencer is almost complete, as well; Jane is just finishing the embroidery. I can't believe she was an apprentice only last year...she has such a deft hand.'

'Then I can wear this to the dance party—perfect,' Mary said happily. Sandrine carefully helped her out of the basted bodice and into her own walking dress. It had also been made by Sandrine, of fine, soft cashmere wool, the duskiest lavender shade edged with silver braid against the chilly, misty winter days.

'We're putting together a party for the theatre,' Mary said as she patted her blonde curls into place. 'It's *The Prophetess*; I know you enjoy Beaumont. Won't you join us? We've taken a box, and Adele would love to see you again. I need someone besides myself for her to prattle on to about her new London wardrobe!'

'I would love to see her, but I'm not sure...' Sandrine began. She did go out in Society at times, to the Pump Room and assemblies, to a private party once in a while. It had become necessary for her business, as people liked seeing an elegant 'French' lady and imagining they, too, could become perfect Parisians with the right gown. But what she much preferred was to retreat to her cosy house in Camden Place after working at the shop, to lock the door behind her, light her fire, pour a brandy, and just breathe. She had worked so hard to build that peace for herself.

Yet—it was true she did enjoy the theatre. She loved losing herself in the poetry and emotion and drama that was not her own. Loved seeing the costumes, the people in the other boxes. And time with Mary, Charles, and Adele was always enjoyable. 'Perhaps, yes.' She reached for a tasselled bell-pull.

Jane, the seamstress, brought in the tea cart with a shy smile, and Sandrine poured out the Darjeeling, arranged the little cakes of pale pink, blue and sage-green, which were the shop's trademark colours. She sometimes wondered if ladies came for the refreshments, the aqua-blue china and fine Indian tea, as much as the gowns.

'Oh, please do! It should be quite a merry evening.' Her expression changed, her smile sliding into teasing. 'And Lord Charlecote will be there. He asks after you so very often since you met him last year. Ella and I find him quite nice, and he must have excellent taste if he admires *you*. He was so lonely after his wife died, and the agency has been trying so hard to help him.'

Sandrine laughed nervously. It was true that Lord Charlecote, the 'nice' widower, was a handsome man still, beautifully dressed, very attentive. Maybe *too* attentive? Ever since they had met at a dinner party at Mary's house, where they were seated together and spoke of books and art, he had made his admiration clear. But something still held her back from forming attachments.

Still, when he asked if he could call on her, she had to admit she'd been tempted. Having someone admire her, be interested in spending time with her, was flattering. She did like her independent life, cherished her quiet time, but that didn't mean she sometimes felt rather—lonely. Didn't sometimes wonder what it would feel like to again be touched, kissed, caressed. To be thought beautiful. After all, she had once been swept away by such glorious pleasure…

No. She shook her head firmly, trying to cast out any thought, any image of Alain, as she always did when he returned to haunt her. When she found herself followed by memories of his smile, his touch, his dark grey, stormy-sea eyes, she jumped even further into work to drive him away.

She feared that no man, even if she dared let one close, could compare to how she had once felt with Alain. He had gone away travelling after they parted so soon after their ill-fated wedding, to Italy, Egypt, maybe Greece…she knew not where. He was building his own business, forging his own path, as she was, independent of their families. She could not have contacted him even if she wanted to. The more time that passed, the more she feared his memory rather than less, the more she thought of him.

And she could not let any man know her secrets. Not let any man hurt her again or make her feel small.

She busied herself with the tea things, trying to

cover her thoughts. 'He does seem very nice, Mary.' She did not mention the vague disquiet she sometimes felt in his presence. Surely, if Mary liked him, Sandrine was imaging things? 'But you know I could not possibly think of marriage.'

Aside from protecting her heart, she was already married, try as she might to forget that fact.

Mary laughed. 'Oh, Sandrine, who said anything about marrying? I am finding it to be a surprisingly delightful state to be in, but it's not for everyone, much as the world tries to persuade us it must be. If you like Lord Charlecote, enjoy his company a little. Let him flirt a bit with you! You are a very beautiful lady who brings such joy to so many with your creations, you deserve a little fun in return.'

Sandrine threw up her hands. 'Fun? What is that? I hardly remember such a word.'

'Exactly. So come to the theatre with us.'

Sandrine suddenly decided that she *would* go. Mary was right. A little fun never hurt anyone. 'Very well. I will!'

Mary smiled in smug happiness, and they took more tea, chatted more about upcoming parties, new fashion papers Sandrine had received from Paris, Adele's plans for London. By the time Mary departed, it was growing dark outside, and Sandrine set about closing the shop after the sales staff had gone. She drew the blue satin draperies, closed the shutters, tidied the glass cases of ribbons and feathers and lace, smoothed the gowns on the mannequins. It was her great pride, that shop;

she had worked so hard to build every gleaming inch of it. Was it enough? It had to be. And usually it was.

Bath was lovely in the winter, the honey-coloured walls veiled in lacy snow, the light diffused and pale golden as it fell over the roofs and railings, the wide greens, the glimpse of the river beyond. She'd been happy there, had made a home for herself. Today it seemed even brighter, sharper.

She smiled and hurried her steps when she glimpsed her little house at the end of the lane. It was nothing grand, just a narrow townhouse of pale cream stone in a row of them, but it was all hers, her sanctuary. Like the shop, she'd worked hard to build it.

Mrs Perkins, her gem of a housekeeper, opened the door, seemingly always knowing when Sandrine was approaching at the end of her workday. Golden light spilled out onto the front steps, turning the stone into a glittering treasure, welcoming her.

'*Madame,*' Mrs Perkins said, a smile lightening her stern-looking face beneath her lace cap. 'We're very glad to see you. It looks as if it might snow tonight.'

Sandrine glanced up at the darkening sky before she stepped inside that light, and unbuttoned her fur-edged pelisse. The black and white tiled hallway led to doors to the drawing room and dining room beyond, a narrow staircase winding up to the bedchambers, and to her little painting studio. It was not fashionably decorated, but crowded with books and old furniture of dark wood and deep cushions, paintings and vases from her parents' house, bric-a-brac brought back from

France, from visits to her mother, who had retired to Brittany after her father died. All just as *she* wanted. Her very own.

'All the better for a nice, cosy fire, then, Mrs Perkins,' she said cheerfully, handing her pelisse, matching little fur hat, and gloves to the housekeeper. 'How were things today?'

'Very peaceful, *madame*. Mrs Smythe has cassoulet for dinner, and a raspberry trifle, when you are ready.'

'*Merci*. In an hour will suit. I'll be staying at home this evening.' Christmas had been a busy season for the shop, and now it looked as though, with Mary in Bath, there would be more social invitations. A chilly evening at the warmth of her own table sounded delightful, as did her cook's raspberry trifle.

She made her way into the drawing room, where a fire did indeed crackle and dance merrily in the grate, illuminating the green walls and yellow-striped curtains, the shelves of leather-bound books, an open sketchbook on the table. A stack of letters waited, bills that needed to be seen to, orders that needed response, probably even a letter from her mother that deserved an overdue answer. She sat down in her favourite faded tapestry armchair by the fire and reached for the papers, but her thoughts drifted far away and couldn't quite be summoned back.

It was lost in that image of Alain that came back to haunt her too often, of his dark grey eyes, his crooked smile. The way his touch had felt on her skin.

She tried so hard, so very hard, never to think of

him. Never to think of that dreadful mistake she'd made when she was too young and sheltered to know better, to see how to protect herself. Sometimes, though, he came flying back to haunt her, so vivid and real.

Where was he now? What was he doing? His parents had since died, and Catherine d'Alency had married, she knew that much. And Alain himself had been away from England for years, travelling, working, building his own life. She did not know where he went. Sometimes she imagined him at ancient temples, crumbling pyramids, golden castles. Places where he seemed to belong.

Her own mother, happily settled in her little château in Brittany after her husband's death, didn't seem to care where Sandrine lived. She had the 'Comte d'Alency' to claim as a relation, which took her far in her own local Society. Sandrine wrote to her mother sometimes, starting after she had found a place at Madame Feydeau's shop in Brighton years ago where she could learn the *modiste*'s trade, learn to translate what she had learned of colour and texture and fabric in her father's warehouses into sellable creations. Her mother assumed she lived in Bath now 'for her health', and thus not always with her husband as he travelled and built his fortune, and that seemed to satisfy her.

Sandrine laughed. In a way, of course, she *was* in Bath for her health. To build up her life again, maintain her serenity. Her mother did not need to know the secrets Sandrine held so close. And the money from her inheritance from her grandmother, the interest, still appeared. She assumed the same with Alain's funds from the marriage settlement. He had what he had needed from her. She had to forget him.

She heard the patter of quick, light steps on the staircase outside the drawing-room door, and put down the letters. She had just risen and turned towards the doorway with a smile when a little girl burst in. A little girl with glossy dark curls and dark grey eyes like her father. A father she had been told travelled a great deal and so could not be with them.

She dashed across the pastel-floral carpet and threw her arms around Sandrine's waist, hugging her tight, which was her customary greeting. Sandrine felt peace and contentment flow through her at that touch. 'Marie! *Ma chère*, how was your day?'

'*Maman!*' Marie cried, her voice touched with a French lilt at the edges. 'You are here at last! My day was splendid, I have so much to tell you…'

Chapter Seven

'I absolutely *must* have my wedding gown from Madame Dumas's shop! Everyone says so,' Françoise cried.

'Hmm?' Alain barely glanced up from his papers, accustomed by now to his sister's sudden great enthusiasms. Françoise had always been lively, mischievous, restless, but had only become more so since she became engaged, and her fiancé left for Paris on a diplomatic mission before the wedding. Ever since she'd left Catherine's house in Derbyshire ('too many babies there, *mon frère*, crying all the time!' Francoise had said), and come to stay with Alain there had been no end to high jinks.

He had thought a stay in Bath might settle things a bit. Bath was not precisely in the first stare of high-flying fashion, yet there was plenty to keep Françoise occupied and out of too much trouble. Shops, theatres, the Assembly Rooms. She'd made plans for them all, but her main concern was building her trousseau. As a diplomat's wife, she declared, she had to be a Lady of Style! A paragon of beauty!

Alain would have thought she was well on her way to that, judging by the piles of hatboxes and trunks in their rented house on Milsom Street. Now, though, her concern was her wedding gown, and this Madame Dumas that everyone seemed to chatter about. Her shop was apparently so exclusive that one had to have an appointment to even visit, to have one's name on a long list for one of those magical gowns.

'Alain!' Françoise cried. She tossed an embroidered pillow at his head, creasing his papers. 'Are you even listening? Don't you care at all? One would think you never missed us one whit!'

Alain laughed as he studied his sister across the sea of hatboxes. She was flopped over the settee, her arms flung dramatically wide, her blue skirts crumpled, not at all like a sophisticated lady in a diplomatic court.

Oh, how he *had* missed them during his travels, his adventures! His sweet, funny sisters. From Istanbul to Athens to Venice to Cairo to Marrakech, he'd revelled in their letters, delighted in finding just the right gifts to send back to them. All his work while he was away, building his career, making his fortune, was for them. He'd made so many mistakes, hurt too many people. He had to make up for it all now.

And then there was Sandrine, the most innocent of all, the one he had hurt the most.

He sighed and put away the paperwork before him. When his mother died recently, several years after his father, who had barely made it past Alain's wedding, he had known he had to come back to England. Catherine had married her vicar, and did indeed have several babies now, and Françoise was engaged to a man whose work took him travelling nearly as much as Alain, but who had a stellar reputation among the diplomatic circles and who had a glowing future, as well as an obvious adoration for his fiancée. Alain knew well that the engagement could not have come at a better time. Françoise would no longer have to be stuck at the house in a little Lake District village where she'd lived with their mother. Her letters burst with life and frustration.

So here they were, in Bath. After all his years of roaming, of snowstorms and sunstruck summers, he had to think of assemblies and wedding gowns. It was quite wonderful.

But it was so, so far above his head.

'Of course I am listening, Françoise,' he said. 'You want a wedding gown from this Madame...'

'Madame Dumas! I've seen some of the ladies here wearing her creations since we arrived, and I have never seen anything so exquisite. Such colours, and lines that make all the ladies look so slim and tall! I know it's because she is French. You can tell by how elegant every lady looks in her gowns, so unique.'

Alain shook his head. 'Françoise, almost every *modiste* from Lands End to John o'Groats claims to be French.'

'But she really is! My new friend Adele has met her several times, even has a gown by her, and says there is no doubt she is French. Maman always said a

French lady innately knows style and elegance at her very core. She's born with it.'

Alain thought of Sandrine, the graceful way she had moved, the way she had used colour and texture and line to show her thoughts and dreams. He hoped she'd had the chance to see those dreams come true, as he had seen his. How he wished he could see her now, but she deserved peace, her own life. He owed her that. 'Just like you and Catherine.'

'So, if I am to be truly elegant, truly make my James proud, I need to stun everyone who sees me walk down the aisle.'

'You could wear a potato sack and everyone would be stunned.' The one time Alain met James in London, to hear the young man's plea for Françoise's hand, he thought he'd rarely seen anyone so infatuated. James and Françoise had looked at each other as if there were no one else in the world, had secret smiles, little jokes they shared. It was enviable indeed, something he'd once longed for himself. Something he'd almost had, if only...

He shook himself out of his thoughts and focused on his sister.

Françoise smiled now, that tiny, soft, dreamy little grin she got whenever she thought of her husband-to-be. 'He is the most darling man in all the world! But I want him to feel like the luckiest man ever, to see the envy everyone has for him to possess such a wife. It would help him so much in his career, to have a wife everyone finds charming.' She punched at the pillow next to her. 'But they say it would be impossible to commission such a gown for at least a year, Madame Dumas is so busy! *Everyone* wants one of her gowns. I've already waited so long for my wedding.'

Alain's heart ached for the sadness he saw in his sister's eyes, the longing to begin her new life, her new family. He remembered such feelings too well. He sat down next to her and wrapped his arm around her shoulders as she leaned against him. 'What about Madame Lescaut? Or Mrs Fisher? I hear they are fashionable. Or that *modiste* who made Catherine's gown?'

Françoise frowned. 'Catherine is a country vicar's wife now! And she is such a great beauty, it doesn't matter what she wears. I need all the help I can find.'

'That is not true at all, nor does James think so,' Alain protested. 'You are very beautiful. Very *French*.'

'My sweet brother.' Françoise kissed his cheek. 'How I missed you.'

'And I missed you. More than I could ever say.' He held her close, wishing the long years he'd been away from his family could be erased. Now he had what he'd so restlessly sought: security for his family. His parents had been comfortable in their last years; Catherine was able to marry the poor vicar she loved. And he had work that made him useful, that gave him a purpose. He wished he could atone for his treatment of Sandrine, tell her of what he'd seen, what he regretted. But where was she? 'But I am here now, and we will make sure you have the most beautiful wedding ever.

There are many fashionable dressmakers out there; we will find just the right one.'

Françoise sighed. 'There are. But there is real *magic* in Madame Dumas's gowns. I just want James to be so proud of me on that day.'

There was such sadness in her voice, something subdued that was not like his mischievous sister at all. He only wanted to make it right for her, make everything right. 'Then we must see what we can do. Where can I find this Madame Dumas?'

'Really, Alain?' Françoise sat up straight, hope lighting her eyes. 'You will help me?'

'If I can. If you promise no more pranks!' He feared his sister was quite as naughty as she'd ever been.

She solemnly clasped her hands to her heart. 'I vow it! Oh, Alain, I only want a wedding that is romantic and grand. Like the ones Maman used to tell us about, of royalty at Versailles! Catherine's wedding was so tiny, barely a ribbon or a flower. Not since yours have I seen—oh!' She clapped her fingers over her mouth, her eyes wide and cheeks pink. 'Oh, no. I am so sorry. I should not have mentioned it.'

Alain took her hand and gave it a reassuring squeeze. Everyone had very carefully *not* mentioned Sandrine or that short-lived marriage since he'd returned to England. He'd told everyone she preferred to live in France with her mother until they could be properly settled, but he sensed they had never believed that.

And he'd also spent years trying not to think of

it, but it was always, always there, in the back of his thoughts, filling his soul.

Not a day had gone by, whether he was in Istanbul or Venice, that he did not remember Sandrine. Didn't see her smile, hear her voice—low, musical, touched with a faint French accent. Not a day he didn't want to talk to her, share something with her of the wonders he'd seen. Not a day he didn't miss her, miss her artistic way of looking at the world around them. Not a day he did not regret.

He'd once been a rash young fool, handed a rare pearl he couldn't even begin to appreciate, and now she had vanished beyond all his attempts to find her. Aside from a few scattered messages over the years, left with his attorney in London, assuring him she was well and nothing else, he didn't know where she was or what she did. He owed her that freedom and peace, after everything.

But oh, how he longed to see her just once more! To look into her jewel-green eyes and tell her, show her, how very sorry he was. How he had changed, and if there was just one more chance…

What would he say? How could he ever persuade her he was sorry for his heedless behaviour? There was really no way he could make up for such stupidity.

He realised he'd been silent too long, lost in the past, in regrets, when Françoise nudged his shoulder. 'I am sorry, Alain. I didn't mean to make you sad.'

He kissed her cheek. 'How can I be sad, when my

beautiful sister is about to take the courts of the Continent by storm?'

Françoise giggled. 'Not just yet! James is just an adjutant right now. But one day he is sure to have his very own consulate.'

'With you to help him, how can he help it?'

'I know, yes? But, Alain, have you not talked to Sandrine all this time? Tried to make things up with her? She did seem so nice.'

He shook his head. 'I owe her whatever freedom she desires. I, and our parents, used her shamefully for her parents' fortune. I do receive messages sometimes that she is well. That's all she owes me.'

'But Catherine and I liked her so much. She was sweet and funny. We wanted to know her better.'

'Sweet and kind. Yes, she was.' He still dreamed of her laughter on cold, quiet nights, her smile, the fire in her when she spoke of art.

'We were shocked you parted so soon.' She leaned closer and whispered, 'Was it because of Danielle Aurac?'

Alain looked at her in shock. 'You know of her?'

'I know you were once infatuated with her. Who could blame you? She was so beautiful. And the way you looked at her…' She frowned at him. 'I was young, but I could see it. I know our parents would never have countenanced such a match.'

'No, they would not. They seemed to think we were still at Versailles.' And now, with all those years behind him, all that experience and study and thought, he couldn't be sure they were wrong to protest after all. Danielle had married her Lord Darby, a wealthy man years older than herself, and gone away with him to his country estate. Since Monsieur Aurac had died and the school was sold, Alain never heard of her, not even through his friend Louis and his new wife. So many disappearances in life.

Now, when he did think of Danielle, he remembered that heady, youthful infatuation, the excitement of her great beauty and mysterious manner. But it was all behind a veil, a haze of anger and regret. The realisation of so much wasted time. The way that youthful blindness had cost him the fledgling marriage he might have had with Sandrine. The time with Danielle felt like a play he had seen once, a farcical scene that had happened to someone else. Far away.

'None of that matters at all now, Françoise,' he told his sister, and it was true that it did not. Danielle and Sandrine were both gone. And he was a different man. 'What matters now is finding a way to get you into *madame*'s salon, if that's what you really, truly want.'

Françoise clapped her hands in glee. 'It is! Oh, Alain, if anyone can get us in there it is you. No lady has ever been able to resist your gorgeous face.'

He laughed, and was afraid he felt a blush heating his cheeks. He ducked away before she could see and tease him about it. 'Not now. I look like a pirate after all my travels. I need a shave and a good tailor.' He ran his hand over the rough whiskers of his jaw.

'You are a rather fuzzy bear at the moment,' Françoise conceded with a laugh. 'But that is easy to remedy. I know what you must try. I just need to find a way...'

Alain did not trust that gleam in his sister's blue eyes. It always meant trouble was imminent. 'What is it?'

'Adele invited us to join her family in their box at the theatre, and they are friends with Madame Dumas! She is sure to be there. I'm sure you could gain an introduction, if you tidy up your hair and beard a bit. Between us we can surely persuade her we would be the best of customers. That I am in dire need of help only she can give us. It will be easy!'

Alain was not at all sure. He was also not yet ready for proper Society on the scale his sister desired; he was too caught up in business now. But Françoise's face was alight with hope, and he couldn't bear to disappoint her.

'Very well,' he said. 'The theatre it is.'

She hugged him in exuberant delight. 'Oh, Alain, *cher frère*! It will work, I am sure. Now, whatever should I wear to the theatre?'

Chapter Eight

'Isn't it beautiful, Alain?' Françoise exclaimed as they made their way into the foyer of the Theatre Royal, with its red velvet and gilt everywhere and a glowing chandelier high overhead casting its light over the silken crowd below. She even spun in a little circle to take in the lights, the marble pillars, the bright crowd that swirled around them.

Alain laughed in delight at his pixie-ish little sister's glee. How he had enjoyed being with her again! She made him remember there could be some fun in life, which he had forgotten in his constantly moving life, his sea of regrets. 'Quite lovely. But not half as pretty as you. No building could ever compare, no matter who made your gown.'

'You are making fun of my enthusiasm,' she chided. She took his arm as they moved further into the crowd, towards the staircase that led up to the boxes. 'I dare say nothing in Bath could match what you have seen on your travels. But after being cooped up so long with Catherine and her brood, watching her so disgustingly in love with Richard and the babies, it all looks like a palace to me. And so many people!'

'Paris and Florence have many very beautiful sites, it's true,' Alain said. 'This compares well to them, I'm sure. Look at that mural over there! And Mrs Giddings' acting has admirers even there.'

Françoise sighed. 'I'm glad we shall see her tonight, then, so I shall have something to talk about when James takes me to London theatres. I should hate for everyone to laugh at his provincial wife!'

'They would never dare. You are a beautiful French lady, a *comte*'s daughter. They'll be falling over themselves to meet you.'

She laughed merrily. 'Oh, Alain, you are the best of brothers! And quite a beauty yourself, especially with your new haircut and your sun-browned air of adventure. You're becoming like a character in a novel! All these ladies cannot keep their eyes off you.'

'Now you're the fanciful one.'

'Indeed I am not! Look around at everyone watching you. I have become an excellent watcher of people—there is little else to do in Catherine's village—and I see very well what happens when I walk down the street with you. Or into a theatre.' She gestured around with her folded fan. Alain studied the space she took in with her gesture, and saw to his surprise it was true. More than a few ladies perused him over their fans, through their opera glasses.

He laughed and ruefully ran his fingers through his hair until he remembered Françoise's admonitions not to muss his carefully-arranged curls. Alain had certainly always admired and liked women, enjoyed their company, their conversation and insights as much as their perfumes and alluring smiles. He certainly hadn't lacked for potential female attention on his travels. Yet somehow, after Sandrine, after kissing her, making love with her, he'd lost that knack for flirtation that once came as easilyy as breathing. It wasn't as fun any more. It could not quite compare.

It was true. No woman he'd met over the years, in Florence, Madrid, Cairo, was equal to that memory that was with him always. That image of her smiling up at him in bed, tousled, enticing. She'd done something to him back then, cast some spell, and now no lady was quite the same. He'd so resented being pushed into a marriage before he was ready, but he'd come to see that Sandrine had been pushed into it as well, when they were young and new to the world. Sometimes he wondered what might have been if they'd met later, had more time…

Sandrine was always there in the darkest, starless hours of a purple-black dusty night sky over Andalusia, in the bitter-sweetness of a coffee in Lyon, the silence of a grand cathedral in Rome. In the beauty of a sunrise, the smell of a sudden rainstorm. A stretch of pure white beach leading to a sunset.

Françoise skipped ahead of him, vivid and golden. If she was a thunderstorm over Livorno, Sandrine had been like a sunset: quiet, serene, pastel-pink. Deceptive. Layers lurking underneath, bright colours, changeable clouds. People would never have guessed that of Sandrine Jaubert. But she really was secrets and mysteries and beauty and art; she needed no one else, for she was all and all in herself as a cat. Like no one he had ever known before or since.

No wonder his youthful self couldn't fathom her then. He'd been so sure he'd known what he wanted. But that was wrong. He'd had exactly what was real within his grasp for one instant, but then she was gone and he was alone.

He could never have followed her. He and his family had used her badly, and she deserved nothing but her own life. But it didn't stop that longing.

'See Lady Petersham over there, Alain?' Françoise said, bringing him back from the cloud-quiet of his regrets and into the crowded theatre. It seemed even more teeming than before, and Alain and Françoise were jostled ahead towards the glass door leading to the theatre itself. 'And Mrs Butler, in the green and gold gown? I heard they have been asking about you most particularly.'

Alain examined the ladies she pointed out. They were indeed pretty, with admiring smiles and little nods, and he wondered if some of his old confidence was coming back with a bit of practice. He laughed at himself.

'A woman could be Aphrodite herself, Françoise, but you do forget one thing…' he said.

Her lips pursed. 'There is a Madame la Comtesse. I do not forget.'

'Yes. I am a married man.'

'Yet you will not bring her here!' Françoise lowered her voice to a whisper. 'And I doubt any of those ladies watching you now would try to drag you down the aisle. A bit of fun with a companion you like could do you some good. Or show you what you should do, if you can get it through your wooden head! Surely we can worry about heirs and such later.' Her expression softened. 'I only want you to be happy, Alain. Whatever that takes. You deserve it.'

But he feared he did not deserve it at all. He'd thrown away a chance for happiness, and now it was always beyond his reach.

He would not ruin Françoise's fun evening for anything at all with his dark thoughts, so he took her arm again and led her onward. 'Refreshments before we find your friends? Lemon squash?'

'I'd rather have champagne,' she said with a laugh. At Alain's shocked glance, she laughed even harder. 'I am a grown lady now, Alain, an engaged lady! I can have champagne, and that is what I want.'

'Anything you wish.' Alain felt such a pang at the reminder that his sisters were grown now, and he was older, too.

As they joined the queue for refreshments, Françoise found a few of her new friends and moved away with them, chatting and laughing. Alain took their glasses of champagne from the footman, and turned to look for her through the crowd.

He found *her* instead.

Despite the press of the people around him, he could suddenly see only one person. The light from the chandeliers, sparkling silver-white, collected around her. She wasn't the tallest lady there, or one of the golden beauties who were the latest fashion. She was of medium height, though she seemed taller, more slender than was stylish, her willowy angles set off perfectly by a gown of dark pink edged with black velvet, simple and stark.

She stood with her back to him in the center of a most animated group, her head tossed back on a laugh. The shallow little vee at the back of her neckline showed the creamy skin of her shoulders, the gold bracelets at her upper arms. She barely seemed to move, the most graceful little shift, a sip of champagne, a flutter of a feathered fan, yet somehow she seemed to rise and float.

Her hair, dark with a faint red sheen, was piled high in almost unruly waves, as if they might soon tumble down. One long curl swung against her white throat and she tossed it back. Against the frills and lace of the other ladies, she looked like a forest nymph, elegant and effortless. And strangely familiar.

A forest nymph.

The champagne glass Alain was raising to his own lips froze. No. No, it could not be her, that was not possible. She was surely somewhere far away, and all his thoughts of her were simply summoning her up in his mind. Everything was set in a whirl of confusion, hope, dread.

She glanced back over her shoulder as if she sensed his attention. Luckily, she did not seem to see him yet, and he had a moment to cover that first, freezing shock, to put the glasses down on a nearby table before he dropped them. It *was* her. Sandrine. His wife, right there in the same room. Even after all the years apart, all those imaginings and dreams, he'd hoped, known, he would find her again. Just not now, not here.

He slid back into the shadows at the edge of the space so he could watch her for just a moment more. His young bride had been so pretty, but this Sandrine, almost five years later, was a goddess. Filled with sophisticated elegance, beauty, perfection. And yet, behind all that perfection was a new coolness. A guarded air, a watchfulness Sandrine had not possessed. Her old sweetness was not there. That easy smile of such sunshine-warmth was gone and he longed for it. Longed to run to her, throw himself at her feet, summon up that heat he'd once so craved.

A gentleman joined her, and kissed her hand. She smiled at him, and it was obvious they knew each other. Alain felt a stab of jealousy he had no right to when he saw it.

He watched her turn to the people gathered beside her, say something that made them laugh. How she had blossomed. From a pretty, shy girl to a creature of sensual beauty and perfect poise, glowing with laughter. Everyone in her circle turned towards her, listened to her, as flowers to the sun. She was the centre of it all, the centre of that man's close attention.

But Alain could only remember who she once had been, who they once were together. The unexpected passion of their wedding night. A familiar heated tightness took hold of him, so inconvenient, and he realised he still wanted her. His own wife, after all this time! He'd wandered thousands of miles, seen pyramids and medieval ruins and oceans, to try to forget what had happened between them, and now one glimpse and he was lost again. As if no time had passed at all. It was the same, the oval cameo of her face, the bright green eyes. Older, more sharply carved, even more beautiful. Everything but her vanished.

He took another glass of champagne from a page's tray and gulped it down, trying to douse that heat, that need to hold her, to smell her rosy perfume again, to *feel* her. No matter how close she was, that could not be again. He had hurt her too much, ruined too much.

She pressed her hand lightly to the man's sleeve, making him lean close to listen to her. There was that cold jealousy again.

She suddenly glanced over, directly at Alain, and she, too, froze. Her laughter faded completely, her face turned snow-white. She swayed, and her companion caught her arm. He stared down at her with a concerned frown, spoke to her, and she shook her head.

Alain tried to vanish into the crowd, to leave her alone to her life as he'd done for so long, but it was all too late. She was walking towards him, slowly, implacably, with a measured, alluringly graceful sway that made her changeable silk skirts shimmer.

She smiled, but it did not reach her eyes. It was cool, polite, mask-like. How he missed the way she had used to smile, filled with joy and enthusiasm. Had he lost her that?

'Sandrine,' he said. It was the only word he seemed to know.

'Alain,' she said quietly. Her voice was lower, that French accent stronger at its edges. But her perfume was the same, rosy and summery. 'I am surprised to see you here. Bath must be so—prosaic after your travels.'

He was startled. 'You know of my travels?'

'Of course! Did you not know that they speak of you in the gossip papers? The dashing *comte* and his thrilling adventures! I have read of it.'

'Have you?'

'Of course. I am as curious about the lands you've visited as anyone else. Alas, I have only travelled to Paris lately! Your travels do sound thrilling.' But her voice was cool, her expression distant, as if nothing he did could ever thrill her at all.

'Thrilling?' Alain managed to laugh. 'It was mostly days of tedium and then ten minutes of danger. But I did see some beautiful sites.' None as beautiful as Sandrine. He could still not believe she was really there, close enough to touch.

She glanced past him, seeming distracted. 'I should like to hear more of it. I always thought you would do something extraordinary.'

'Did you think so?' he asked hoarsely. Had she

thought of him over the years, missed him at all? He wanted to ask, to demand she tell him, but he also did not really want to know. She could very well have never thought of him at all. But there was a tension just beneath her coolness.

'How could I not have?'

Her friends were watching them with avid curiosity on their faces. The man who had stood with her seemed taut with anger. She made no move to draw him closer to them, to introduce them. What could they say to each other, anyway? How could they ever enter each other's world now?

Alain sensed their moment was drawing short. 'Can I meet with you alone, Sandrine?' he said quietly, suddenly rather desperate not to lose her again.

A frown flickered over her brow. She opened her rosy-gold lips, as if she would refuse. Alain dared to take a step closer, to even brush his hand against hers, under cover of a silken fold of her skirt. She shifted, moved away, her glance falling, and he felt that old heightened awareness of flirtation, pursuit, come over him. But this was *Sandrine*.

'Please,' he whispered.

Her gaze flew up, and she stared steadily into his eyes. Finally, she nodded. 'Very well. Shall we walk in Sydney Gardens tomorrow? It is quieter this time of year than the Pump Room would be.'

'Thank you,' he said simply. He had a day to discover what to say, what would begin to make it up to her. But really, what could possibly make up for what he had done to her? He only knew the burning need to see her again, to discover the Sandrine he had once known, and hoped was still there.

He gave her a bow, resisting the urge to take her hand, to press a kiss to her fingers, breathe in deeply of that perfume. He had to move slowly, carefully, not startle her away. She watched him with the wariness and delicacy of a forest creature on the verge of fleeing. He knew how to bide his time.

She swirled around, graceful and light, and glided back to her friends. The man she was with took her arm, leaned close to speak in her ear. Alain felt a stab of cold, unfathomable jealousy. She just shook her head and gave a small smile.

'That is her, isn't it? Madame Dumas?' Françoise said, bouncing up to his side. 'I saw you talking to her! Do you know her? From before?'

Alain took his sister's arm and led her towards the staircase. 'It turns out that I did once know her, yes.' He decided he had to be honest. Soon enough there would be no hiding the truth from Françoise. 'She was once known as Sandrine Jaubert.'

Françoise gasped, her eyes as large as saucers. She stepped back, her gloved fingers clasped to her mouth. 'Your—your *wife*? Oh, Alain! How...?'

'We should not talk of it here,' he said sternly. 'I do not know very much. Don't breathe a word of it to anyone yet. It is clear she's made a new life for herself here in Bath, and I owe her not to create a scandal that could jeopardise that.' A life as a renowned modiste. He would have imagined her an artist, painting her glorious canvases, but perhaps gowns and hats were her art now. A disguise. It seemed to work; people gravitated towards her here, just as he once had. As he still did.

Françoise nodded, but her eyes were still huge with curiosity. 'Of course. I just…'

Alain's eyes narrowed. 'Just what?'

'I am not planning a mischief, I promise! It is just, since we know her, do you think I could persuade her to make me a gown after all?'

Alain sighed, and pinched the bridge of his nose. He needed patience. 'You are utterly incorrigible.'

'It must run in the family.'

Why was he here? *Why was he here?*

Sandrine tried to laugh and talk as if she were having a grand time as she settled into her red velvet seat in Mary's box. To wave her fan, gossip about the play, the crowd around them, for after all it was that crowd that kept her salon so busy. They could never, ever find out the truth.

Yet she was constantly, achingly aware of Alain in a smaller box near theirs. She did not see anything but him in the full theatre, as if a footlight glowed only on him. He hadn't grown stout or bald as some men did over the years. He was even stronger, leaner, his skin sun-browned from his travels, his dark hair lighter.

He was always god-like handsome, of course, strong, beautiful, but now he was so much *more*. The years, his travels, had hardened him, sharpened his youthful beauty. Leaned back lazily in his chair, he was not looking at her but somehow she sensed he was fully aware of her. It was as if a golden cord still bound them together across the distance.

She waved her fan a little faster. Once, as a silly girl, she'd fantasised that she loved him. Until he had shattered her heart. Until she knew he loved another, that he had simply needed the Jaubert fortune and Sandrine was the key to acquiring it.

She was no longer that girl.

At last, the footlights dimmed and he was cast somewhat into shadow. She snapped her fan closed, and turned to face the stage, the scene of the famous Mrs Giddings making her entrance to tumultuous applause before she rushed towards her stage lover. How she'd longed to do just that when she first saw Alain again! So ridiculous. False drama and tears were much easier to think about, but she couldn't quite focus on the play. She fought to keep her dignity, the dignity she'd struggled so hard to find over the years. That carapace of secrets, layers of masks she relied on to live her life. She had a new existence now, reliant only on herself, and one glimpse of him sent it into tatters.

But it could change nothing. *Would* change nothing. She'd built her life; nothing could change it. She had long ago accepted what had happened between them, and it wasn't different now.

Except that suddenly *everything* was different. Alain was back in her life.

And horrors, what if he saw Marie?

A cold rush of nausea rose up in her at that terrifying thought. Her daughter! She'd protected Marie for so long, her most precious jewel, her baby. Marie believed that her father travelled the world for work. Sandrine had tried to write to Alain when she discovered she was pregnant from their wedding night, but he had already vanished on his constant travels, never staying in one place for long, and it didn't seem right to put such news in brief messages to an attorney. After long enough, she didn't even know how to begin. That fierce protectiveness that had arisen in her when Marie was placed in her arms was too strong.

And that old fear was still there. What if Alain took Marie away? *Mon Dieu*, at least Marie was not a boy, a future *comte*! But there was still danger.

And having come face to face with him again after so long, she saw now he held one further, savage danger. The danger to her own heart.

Chapter Nine

Sandrine loved Sydney Gardens in the winter. The pathways, statues and flowerbeds were layered with frost, sparkling and silvery in the pale yellow sunlight that peeked through the pearl-grey clouds, and only a few hardy souls were out walking. She loved the endless green expanse of it, the paths that could lead anywhere at all, the glimpses of the river and the rolling, shimmering city beyond. In the summer the park was crowded, but in colder months it was almost her own private fairy-land. Her place to be alone, away from the constant demands of the shop, a place to think.

And today those thoughts were filled with nothing but Alain. She'd thought she would never see him again, that he would forever be a memory, growing blessedly hazier over the years, until maybe, just maybe, she'd think of him no more. He would just be part of the old life of Sandrine Jaubert, the life where she had no control. She was Sandrine Dumas now. Alain had no place in that 'now'. He only belonged to 'then'.

But there he was. Suddenly appeared in the *now*. And Sandrine had a problem. So, so many problems.

She wrapped the high sable collar of her ruby-red pelisse closer under her chin, and tugged the matching little fur hat over her ears as the cold wind swirled past. She tucked her gloved hands deeper into her velvet and sable muff, wrinkling up her chilly nose, and hoped he might appear soon. The sooner they talked, the sooner they could go back to their lives. Their separate lives.

She had worked so hard to make a life for herself, to build up contentment and fulfilment, security. It was lonely sometimes, that was true, but at least her heart was safe. Now, just glimpsing his face again, all that old hope and passion and pain came right back.

How she had longed to build herself a stout suit of armour to ward off hurt like that! Meeting him at the theatre, seeing how he had grown even more handsome as the years passed, looking into his dark grey eyes, time seemed to spread out again and cover all else, as if she'd only seen him yesterday.

That was dangerous. She hoped seeing him face to face in the cold light of day, not surprised with his sudden appearance after so long, she'd set things right at last. She would see he wasn't real, he was just a girlhood dream of hers.

She reached the fountain of the hunting goddess, Diana, and drew in a deep, chilly breath to try and clear her head. The children dashing past reminded her of Marie, of all she had to lose if she made a misstep with Alain.

She heard a crunch on the gravel of the pathway, and turned to see Alain making his slow way towards her. She saw at once she had been wrong. Even in that bright light, it hadn't been her imagination at all. Dressed in a fashionable dark blue greatcoat, his face shadowed by the brim of his hat, mysterious, he was just the same storm on the calm waves she'd made of her life.

The years melted away, dissolving from the edges of the ice-bright day, and she remembered how it once had been. Every moment he had looked at her back then, as if he could read her very heart; every touch of his hand, his fingers dancing over her skin, bringing such sizzling pleasures.

She stood up straighter, drew her pelisse closer around her. She had to build her armour again, be rid of that pain she'd fought so hard to banish from her heart. The pain was closing in tight now, barbed with ice.

Yet when he came closer, when she could feel the heat of him on the breeze, smell his clean, lemon scent, it was so much like it had used to be. It made her dizzy. Up close, she could see that he looked a little older, just as she did, with faint lines fanning out from the edges of his night-grey eyes. He was leaner, harder, his gaze cautious, but he was even more handsome. Drat him.

'Sandrine,' he said simply. He gave her a little bow, but he didn't reach for her. He seemed to sense how brittle she felt, how cold. One tiny caress, and she would surely collapse in shards and dust at his feet.

She had to be strong, for Marie. 'I thought you were

in Sienna. Or Nice,' she said. She spun around and walked along the pathway, even as she knew she could never run from him. He fell into step beside her, their strides matched easily, his sleeve brushing hers. She was fully aware of every small movement he made, of the sound of his breath.

'I was. And Rome before that.'

She couldn't stifle the little spark of curiosity. 'Doing what?'

He shrugged. 'Just business. And then the Foreign Office called on me for a little errand in Nice, that's all.'

Which surely meant that, whatever his business was, he didn't want to talk about it. She'd realised that he might take on some government work on his many travels. So different from the careless young Alain she'd known. More solemn, more watchful.

And she—well, of course she was no longer that same naive girl. She'd had such ideas then of how her life would unfold! Now she was a businesswoman, a mother. She couldn't afford to melt for Alain d'Alency again. Couldn't lose her armour.

'Then why Bath now?' she asked. 'How dull it must be after Cairo and Athens!'

'Dull is exactly what I hope for now. Italy has its charms, but peace and quiet isn't usually among them.'

Sandrine sighed. Her thoughts at that moment could not be called *peaceful* at all. 'Peace and quiet we have here in spades, I assure you.'

'Is quiet a benefit to your salon?' he asked curiously. 'I know little of the fashion business, but I would imagine parties and gossip papers and such would be its life-blood.'

'And you would be right. Bath is not London or Paris, but it does attract many ladies of fashion who are always wanting to be stylish and dashing, to be originals. There is not much competition here, and I can learn all the subtleties of my business.'

Find her own peace. That was what she'd worked so very hard for. She couldn't let it go now.

'So you came here to Bath after, well, after we parted, and opened your salon?'

Sandrine laughed. 'I hadn't the first idea how to run a business then! I persuaded another *modiste*, Madame Feydeau in Brighton, to take me on as an assistant. I worked from dawn to dusk to learn all I could about design and business, such as accounts. I was able to live off my grandmother's inheritance, and when this shop in Bath came up for sale it seemed as fine as anywhere else.'

He watched her very closely as she spoke, as he always had, paying attention, listening with an interest few men showed to women's conversation. 'Your gowns, especially your wedding gowns, seem to be very à la mode. Everyone talks of them. Françoise is wild to have one for herself.'

'Your sister?' She remembered his beautiful, kind sisters, who had welcomed her into their home as their brother had not been able to truly do.

'Yes. She is to marry a diplomatic adjutant, which

means she feels she must be seen as extra-fashionable. She is in despair that you seem to have a lengthy waiting list.'

She laughed again, delighted to hear her reputation was growing. 'I do. But bring her to see me. I remember her; she was so pretty and energetic. Like a pixie, or an elf. She must be very lovely indeed now. I'm sure I could do something special for her.'

'She would be in your debt. And I would be in your debt. Or, should I say, even more in your debt.'

She glanced at him, startled at his solemn tone. Had he suffered pangs of guilt, regret over the years, as she had? 'Oh, Alain. We have no debts between us; we have both done what we chose in life, thanks to the bargain we struck.'

And he had given her the greatest gift of all: Marie. She had to tell him—wanted to tell him—but how?

They walked on in silence, the sea of the past between them, stormy, roiling, uncrossable.

'Where shall you go next?' he asked at last, as they came to the stone expanse of a bridge. 'Surely your business will grow beyond Bath. To London, maybe?'

Sandrine bit her lip uncertainly. She had confided her most treasured plan in no one, not even Jane, her trusted seamstress, or Mary Campbell. Somehow, though, it felt as if she could tell him. Maybe it was that careful, sincere interest in his eyes that lulled her into feeling safer.

'I would really like to open a shop in Paris. On Rue de la Paix, maybe. Something achingly elegant, with every luxury, offering the most daring of gowns.' She'd sat awake so many nights, sketching, dreaming. France seemed to call to her, to match with her visions, her ambitions.

He tilted his head as he considered this. 'Paris?'

'Yes. You must think me quite fanciful. I barely remember France from my childhood, and we were cut off from Paris for so long. But when I visited there last year, something in it just seemed to—to fit. Perhaps I am still more French than I thought!'

Alain was quiet for a long moment, studying the ice-choked river thoughtfully. 'Paris is longing for elegance now, for beauty. Ripe for new businesses. Maybe if nothing was available on the Rue de la Paix, you could find a smaller salon near by. Begin with a small, select client list, *très* exclusive. Like your wedding-gown waiting list. Only a few special people can have them. Whet their appetites, just as you have here. Walk in the Jardin du Luxembourg, or ride in the Bois de Boulogne in your finest creations—you are your best advertisement. You *are* your gowns, your style to be emulated. No one could be more elegant.'

Sandrine laughed, and felt the heat of her old girlhood curse, that blush, flood over her face. How his approval had once mattered so much to her! She couldn't let it do so now.

He smiled, a wide, swift white grin of delight, the old, younger Alain emerging. To her shock, he reached up and gently skimmed one gloved fingertip over her cheek, leaving a trail of fire behind. 'I see you still have your blush.'

She fell a step back, struggling not to reach up to scrub the sensation of his touch away—or hold it closer. 'There is not usually time for such things as blushing.'

'Too busy planning for Paris.'

'Yes. I keep sketchbooks of ideas, save every penny.'

'If I can help in any way...'

She shivered at the reminder of what had really always been between them: money. 'No!' she said, more sharply than she'd intended. 'No, I am fine.'

'Sandrine,' he said quietly, the look he slanted down at her tender. 'You helped my family when they were in desperate need. My parents were able to live their last years in comfort and peace. I owe you so very much. I have a large income now thanks to my own work...'

His tone was so earnest, almost hopeful, as if he longed to really repay her what could never be replaced. She felt a softening towards him, against her will. Alain had never been mean, not deliberately cruel, she knew that; he had been heedless, careless, young. Maybe he still wanted to make that up to her in some way. But she couldn't let him. She had too much to lose if she allowed him back into her life now. 'Don't concern yourself, Alain, please. I am fine.'

They walked on, side by side but so far apart. 'I thought that you wished to be an artist. To paint. Your work was so exquisite.'

She flashed him a teasing, masking smile. 'And gowns are not art? My clients would say different.'

He laughed wryly, a dark, rich, warm sound that still washed over her like an island ocean wave. She wished he wouldn't do that; it made her remember too well the bright moments she had once spent with him, the hopes she'd held. 'They must be indeed; they seem so transforming.'

'For good or ill.' She grimaced to think of some of her earliest designs, the garish colours, the overly lavish trimmings. She had learned over the years what suited each woman, what flattered and flowed. 'But yes, I did love painting. I'm surprised you remember that.' Yet once he had understood it so well. She remembered he'd said it seemed as if painting was a part of her. 'But proper art takes time, takes every ounce of patience and passion. I have many responsibilities.'

'As do we all.' They continued on their path. 'Sandrine, surely you see that we can't go on like this, since we have found each other again. I never should have let it go for so long.'

She studied him in confusion at the sudden, serious shift in his tone, the stiff set of his shoulders. She was frightened by it. 'But why? We've done well enough thus far...'

'Because we are married!' he said, exasperated. He kicked at a loose bit of gravel with the tip of his polished boot. 'That is why we cannot go on this way. I have not been a good or kind husband, I know that well. Not any sort of husband at all. It has haunted me.'

Her eyes widened in realisation. 'And you need an heir. A little *comte*.'

His head jerked back as if she'd slapped him. 'I don't care about such things. Only my parents did. Besides, there is only a crumbling château in France to inherit, and no one deserves that trouble. But we *are* married. We need to talk about that.'

And that was the inescapable truth. Sandrine stared hard at the water beyond, the icy-white edges of it, unable to look at him. To let him see the secrets in her eyes. 'What can we have to say about it after all these years?' Except that one thing of greatest importance. Marie.

'Exactly!' he exclaimed. 'Mostly, I must just apologise. Properly. Abjectly. At last.'

Sandrine wondered about his Danielle. His great love. Where was she now? Did he hope to find her again, to make things right with her once he had dealt with his folly of a marriage? 'That is not necessary,' she said, longing to escape from his overwhelming presence, from the park, from herself.

'It is *very* necessary. Please, Sandrine, meet with me again. Somewhere we can be alone and talk.'

To be alone? Oh, how tempted she was! What a pull he still had on her!

It began to snow, a white, lacy flurry that caught on her lashes. The chill of it seemed to wake her up. 'You can bring Françoise to my salon tomorrow. Then we shall see.'

His smile burst forth again, burning through the

snow, burning through her armour. 'Thank you! Françoise will be ecstatic. I am sure—no, I just hope—we can find a way to be friends again.'

Had they ever been *friends*? Sandrine remembered that was what he had once said he wanted, when she discovered he loved Danielle and needed only a convenient marriage. She hated how much that still hurt. 'I must go,' she said. 'I have an—an appointment.'

'Let me escort you…'

She shook her head frantically. She just needed to get away, to think. 'It is not far. I'm going to Mollands, to meet my friends Mary Campbell and Lord Charlecote.'

He frowned. 'The man at the theatre.'

Sandrine was surprised he might know who he was. And—was that a hint of *jealousy* in his voice? She could hardly credit that. 'Yes, he is a friend.' She decided to tease him just a bit. 'I am sure *you* have had friends these many years.'

His face turned rosy, and not from the cold. He scuffed his toe through the trace of snow on the ground. 'That is not the same.'

She laughed. 'Of course not. You are a *man*.' And men had as much freedom as they wanted.

'I have heard that Mrs Campbell and her sister run a matchmaking kind of business. Have they been trying to gain a new client in you, Sandrine?'

She laughed again, feeling rather delighted that he could possibly be jealous. Possibly see her in some new light. 'They cannot, can they? I'm already married, and they only make respectable sorts of matches.'

She walked away, feeling the heat of his gaze watching her go.

Chapter Ten

Sandrine was quite nervous as she opened her salon bright and early the next day. She was doubly careful that every display was straight, every fold of every gown perfect.

'It must be a duchess, at least, who is coming!' Jane whispered to another *vendeuse*.

'No, a queen, I am sure!'

Sandrine had to laugh. She *had* been acting rather wildly, fluttering around here and there, putting out a hat then taking it back, smoothing a skirt over and over. 'The bride is sister to a French *comte*, and engaged to a diplomat, so our designs could be seen all over the Continent. She is also an old friend of mine.'

She remembered Françoise d'Alency and her sister, Catherine. Françoise had been so merry, so elfin and prankish, and Catherine so dignified and lovely. Sandrine wondered what Françoise could be like now, what she wanted from her married life. Sandrine had helped so many brides navigate the first steps of a new life, had hoped her gowns, her advice, could hold them up, give them faith in themselves. Maybe she could do the same for Françoise.

But what would Alain's sister think of *her* now? What had Alain told his family about her?

Sandrine studied the salon, realising that no amount of tidying would steady her nerves now. She'd just tweaked a display of sunset-coloured silk scarves when the little silver bells at the door rang out merrily.

She turned, a careful smile on her lips. Alain stood there, silhouetted by the sunlight outside, his hair tumbling into those same dark curls, a young lady on his arm. She gazed around, wide-eyed with curiosity, and Sandrine had a moment to study her.

Sometimes she was so busy, so occupied with the business and with Marie, the time since she'd had her brief life with Alain seemed not so long ago. Then sometimes it felt an eternity away, and she wasn't sure she hadn't imagined it all.

Now, looking at Françoise d'Alency, she remembered well the young girl who had fluttered so excitedly through Sandrine's wedding breakfast, her bright curls flying, her laughter so loud and free. A part of that world Sandrine had wanted for herself.

But this was a lady who stood before her now. Tall, graceful, those red-gold waves smoothed beneath a little velvet hat. She wore a walking dress and spencer of aqua-blue velvet trimmed with darker blue ribbon, fashionable but not the best colour for her. Sandrine could see right away that a clear greenish-blue would bring out the merry glow in her eyes, the gold in her hair. The latest narrow skirt style from France would also show her slim figure to perfection.

Those were things Sandrine dealt with every day, her expertise, her business. Helping women look and feel their best so they could conquer their lives was what she lived for. But she'd never done it for her own sister-in-law before.

Her *sister-in-law*. Alain's sister! When Françoise turned to look at her, Sandrine almost fell back a step. The same changeable dark grey-blue eyes as Alain, as Marie.

She forced herself to keep smiling, and came forward with her hand outstretched. 'Mademoiselle d'Alency! How lovely to see you again. How you have changed!'

Françoise dropped a little curtsey, strangely uncertain. As if she was struck by the same shyness as Sandrine when faced with the past. 'And you hardly look different at all, Mademoiselle Jau—er—Madame la Comtesse.' She glanced up at Alain. 'It is amazing.'

'Please, do call me Sandrine,' she said slowly. Each word felt like a careful tiptoe-step. 'Come, let me show you the salon. Alain tells me you are soon to be married, and need a fine gown and trousseau.'

Françoise suddenly beamed. 'Yes! He is with the Foreign Service, in Paris at the moment, which is why I am stuck here with my no-fun brother.' She nudged Alain's shoulder, and they grinned at each other, making Sandrine's heart ache. 'Oh, Mademoiselle Jau— Sandrine! He is so very handsome, so smart and kind.

I am very fortunate indeed. Yet...' She glanced at the gown on the mannequin near by, biting her lip wistfully.

'Yet what, Françoise?' Sandrine asked.

'He has a brilliant future ahead, everyone says so. I fear I might let him down, not learn to be a proper partner to him. I've lived so quietly, with my mother and then my sister. You know that Catherine married a vicar? Can you fathom it?'

Sandrine smiled. 'I had heard, yes. I hope she is very happy.'

'Oh, she is, but she is so dull now, with all her children and her parish visits and her ladies' reading group! She has no advice on current fashion for me.'

'Well, you have come to the right place. We help ladies with just such advice every day,' Sandrine reassured her. 'Let me show you a few of our samples, and you can tell me what appeals to you.' She gestured to her *vendeuses*, hovering in the background, watching them curiously. 'Jane, if you could see that the *comte* has a comfortable chair and a glass of wine for a time?'

They all rushed forward eagerly to surround Alain. The ladies always had adored him, and Sandrine saw nothing had changed! They bore him off to a chair, chattering as he cast an imploring look over their heads. Françoise didn't even look at him; no one was rescuing him.

Was that how Danielle Aurac had once been? Maybe still was. Sandrine could not bear to think of that now.

'I was so fascinated to find out the famous *madame*

was really you!' Françoise said, twirling a little with the pale pink gown held against her. 'Everyone said your list was far too long, and I would never be able to order a gown in time.'

'We do have a great many loyal patrons.'

'I can see why.' She reached out to reverently touch a velvet cloak. 'These are so astounding.'

What on earth could Françoise think of her brother's strange marriage? 'Mademoiselle d'Alency...'

'Françoise!'

'Françoise.' Sandrine took a deep breath. 'You must think it so strange that I came to be here in Bath.'

Françoise tilted her head to study Sandrine. 'Living apart from my brother, you mean?'

'Yes.'

She frowned, and carefully laid aside the gown. 'I adore Alain. But even I knew, when I was just a girl, that he would be no easy proposition to live with in an everyday way. He was too headstrong, too—well, a bit self-centred. And his friends, Henri-Robert and Louis—eek. So wild! Both are now married men with lots of children and grown rather stout, *naturellement*.' She glanced around the gleaming shop. 'You had to be free to create this wondrous space, I can tell. It is so very special. But Alain has changed. He is not that careless young rake at all any more, I promise you that. His travels, the things he has seen and learned—how could he help but be different? To have grown?'

Sandrine slowly nodded. She had also seen glimpses

of that in him, in his new, careful way of speaking, the solemn look in his eyes.

Françoise caught up a velvet tippet of rich amethyst-purple and spun around again. 'Ooh-la-la! I do adore this. It's your very own design?'

'Yes, one of my favourites. You see the way the collar is here? It can be worn over a wedding gown on a chilly day as you walk from the church. Like so.' She spun it over her shoulders, suddenly remembering her own wedding day, the wild hopes she'd had then.

'I love it.' Françoise slipped behind the mannequin to study how she might look in the jonquil-yellow dinner gown. 'This is so daring! Just look at this hemline. Yet I fear I could never look right in it. Not like a diplomat's sophisticated wife should.'

'Of course you can! This style was meant for a lively, spirited sort of young bride. And any gown is mainly about the attitude of the lady who wears it. It is like her armour, her disguise. Her way of showing the world who she wishes to be.' Sandrine took the satin gown from the mannequin and held it up to Françoise, adjusting the neckline. 'This colour, this pearly sheen, is perfect for your hair, for your skin tone. It makes you glow, see? Like a—a goddess of the sunrise sky! You can dominate a room without a word said. Just stand there, glance about to meet everyone's eye, and they are yours.'

Françoise laughed in delight. 'It is a costume! In my own play.'

'*Exactement*. The world is your own theatre, and you

can be anyone you like.' Sandrine reached for a spool of beaded lace and draped it over the shoulder of the gown. 'I can help you become a great lady of fashion, to have people adore and look up to you. To teach you to tell your very own story with clothes.'

Françoise glanced at her, suddenly serious. 'As you do, Sandrine?'

'As we all do. Or can. Look at your brother.' She gestured at Alain, who was laughing and entertaining the salesgirls now, making them giggle and ply him with cakes. 'His story says he is careless right now.'

Françoise studied him thoughtfully. 'I see what you mean. He wants to *say* he is careless. But I know—I think you and I both know—he is not at all.' She suddenly took Sandrine's hand in hers. 'I shall never wish to pry into your life, Sandrine. I just want to say we have all missed you very much. Alain has changed so much, he really has.'

Sandrine thought of the beautiful Danielle, of how much he was sure he had loved her then. 'Françoise...'

'Please, do not give up on him. On us. I need your advice so much! And so does Alain, though he might not admit it yet.'

Sandrine smiled at her, a wave of tenderness washing over her, much as it did when she looked at Marie. 'It will be my pleasure to help you however I can, Françoise. I understand your first step is that you require a wedding gown?'

'Oh, yes!' Françoise cried. Her eyes shone with delight. 'Something unlike anything else, something that will astonish everyone when they see me in it.'

'Well, that is my speciality. Come, let's look at some fashion papers and you can tell me what you envision.'

Sandrine led Françoise to one of the blue satin settees dotted around the salon, and took out a pile of French fashion papers for them to look through. As they examined sleeves and trains and veils, she remembered her own wedding. It was a memory she usually tried to push away, to forget, but today, with Alain so close, it was as vivid as yesterday. The smell of the lilies, the nervous flutter in her stomach, the haze of everything through lace. The hope that had bloomed so warm and fresh.

She shook her head to be rid of the old images, and gestured to one of the *vendeuses* to bring some tea. The girl reluctantly left the laughing circle clustered around Alain.

Sandrine turned to one of the latest illustrations. 'This is the latest style in Paris. I think it would suit you very well indeed, though this sleeve—'

'Oh!' Françoise suddenly squeaked. She dug around behind her back, under the braid-edged velvet cushion, and brought out a doll. Its golden curls were tangled, its arm crooked, obviously well-loved. Françoise studied it, bemused. 'Is this a new fashion doll?'

Of course it was not, with its faded lacy skirts and mussed hair. It was Marie's favourite. For a moment, Sandrine could not breathe. She glanced at Alain where he chatted with her shopgirls, and knew she was not nearly ready to tell him what he must know, even though she knew she must. He deserved the chance to know his daughter. She made herself laugh and took it from Françoise to tuck it away in a nearby basket. 'Some patrons so like to bring their children. We sometimes make small fashions, too.'

Françoise sighed wistfully. 'Such lucky little girls!' Fortunately, she seemed to forget the doll immediately, and turned the page of the papers. 'Oh, I do like this one. What a clever sort of layered skirt! Could this part be done in pink?'

'It is your gown,' Sandrine said with a laugh. 'Perhaps I should visit you in your lodgings and bring more samples for us to go over, make a few sketches?' She felt such reluctance to be in Alain's own house, but surely it would be safe enough if she was working, doing what she knew best? She wanted this gown to be the finest she'd ever made; then any debt between her and Alain would be finished, and they could part again. Surely...

Sandrine sat up late that night after Marie was tucked in bed, and sketched by lamplight, trying to lose herself in her work as she so often did. When she was absorbed in line and colour, in trying to make the enticing visions in her head a beautiful reality, she forgot all else. She saw only movement and scenes.

Françoise deserved a glorious gown to begin her new life, and Sandrine had such ideas for her. Flowing tulle, gleaming satin, lace flowers and glittering embroidery. But there, in the quiet darkness of the night, she kept remembering her own gown. The pale, girlish bows along the neckline, the edges of the overskirt sparkling with tiny pearls. It had not been what she would choose now. She was no longer that naive, romantic girl who dared to believe for one wondrous moment in 'love at first sight'.

Or at least, she'd always believed that wasn't her now. She'd made her dream come true, one she'd believed back then could never be. She had her own business, her work, her art. It wasn't painting, as she'd once wanted, but her gowns were art now, and she could use them to help other women find the confidence in themselves she'd once lacked. It was a good life, and Alain had obviously made his own dreams of independence come true as well.

They had no place for each other in their new lives. She'd had to build a protective shell around herself, for her own sake—and especially for Marie's. But now, seeing Alain again, being near him, gave her feelings she'd thought long buried. A sense of lightness, and longing.

And he had changed, too, just as she had. He had grown, hardened. There was a depth to his eyes she'd not seen before.

Maybe, just maybe, they had both changed enough to see how to start again? In a new way?

Sandrine tossed down her pencil and ran her hand over her face, tired and confused and trying to push away any hope that dared creep in. Hope had broken her heart before. She couldn't afford that now.

They did have to make some kind of new beginning, of course, for Marie. He deserved to know the truth, and surely Marie deserved to know her father. It was only right. It scared Sandrine, but she somehow knew it had to be done. Her daughter needed that.

For herself, though…

She pushed away from the desk and went to the window to study the quiet street below. The houses, all pale stone in the starlight, slept behind their curtains, and in the distance she could see the faint ripple of the river. A carriage drew up at the house across the street, and a couple climbed down. They leaned against each other sleepily as they returned from some ball or rout. They paused to kiss, tenderly, wrapped up in only each other.

She felt such a longing for her young love, her young self. The echo of a past that felt endless, where every touch had seemed a promise. If only time would spool back, if only she and Alain had one more chance to love with the wild, unguarded fervour of youth. But she could only move forward now.

Chapter Eleven

Sandrine liked to think of the Assembly Rooms as a sort of second salon of work. She could meet anyone there, current clients who needed new gowns for the next Season, possible clients who needed a boost of confidence, friends and rivals. An evening there always promised such *possibility*. Anyone could be there at all! Anything could happen when all of Bath gathered in the golden candlelight, the swirl of music and laughter.

She might even meet Alain there. But that was not why she dressed with a bit more care and concern that evening, not why she fussed with her hair and the curling tongs a bit longer. Oh, no, no! Never that. She surely did not want him to notice her at all. Everything had become so much more complicated since he had appeared in her life again, so much more confused.

If, however, he *did* see her in her new *à la Diane* gown of deep sapphire blue, it would not be the *worst* thing. If the past had been different, if they had met now instead of then, would things be different?

As Sandrine neared the honey-coloured stone building, glittering in the dusting of new snowfall, with its crush of carriages crowding close, she paused to study the pillared portico she'd entered so many times. Welcoming amber light spilled from the windows as guests eagerly flocked towards its party-promise. She studied the gowns, the fur-edged pelisses and small-brimmed hats, making note of new styles she could try. Ladies who would need her help.

Alain wasn't among the crowds, not yet. She remembered how eager she had been to see him again after their unforgettable first meeting, how she had thrown herself so precipitously into wild emotions, into sparkling hope. How just the thought of him would make her very toes tingle! Now she had to be so careful, to remember Marie, remember the armour of her heart.

She gathered her fur-edged cloak closer around her and joined the flood of revellers making their way towards the elegant, pastel-pink and marble ballroom, the sun-yellow card room, the mint-green refreshment space. She swam through the crowds on the stairs as they called out to each other, kissed powdered cheeks, exclaimed over the crush, the heat. A few patrons eagerly stopped her, and she nodded and chatted and smiled, trying to be subtle, careless, as she looked for Alain.

The river of people spilled in a perfumed wave into the ballroom, crests of white muslin, bright silks, feathers, metallic embroidery, ribbons, all scattered and refracted. The music was beginning, adding its sparkle to the aura of fun.

No Alain yet. She took a glass of wine, and studied the fresh eddies of the crowd swirling past her as she mentally re-designed some of the gowns to flatter the wearers more.

She glimpsed Mary Campbell and her handsome husband, Charles, as they waltzed past on the dance floor. They'd been married for months, and it was quite unfashionable to dance with one's own spouse, but they smiled up at each other in such a palpable sunny glow of happiness that the whole room was blanketed in its warmth. They stared blissfully into each other's eyes, swirling and gliding as one, oblivious to all else. And, if Sandrine did say so herself, Mary's pale green gown looked quite superb, adding to that Goddess of Joy glow.

For a moment, she dared let herself imagine dancing with Alain like that. Floating in his arms across a dance floor, held close to his heart, his strength. Eyes only for one another, no past, no future to dread.

She turned away from the dancing couples and reached for more wine as she snapped her fan open with one hand, telling herself sternly that she was not the dreamy girl she had once been. Surely, if she reminded herself of that enough, it would sound true.

Suddenly, as if he was summoned by her daydreams of him, she glimpsed him through the crowd. As beautiful as a god, striding ahead in the world that belonged only to him.

Her painted-silk fan waved just a bit faster against

her heated cheeks. He disappeared behind a column, and she spun away.

Lord Charlecote appeared beside her, bowing and smiling. She remembered what Mary said about him, that he often asked after her, and she wished she could have found a man like him when she was young, fallen for him as she had for Alain. He seemed so steady, so settled in life, and maybe her own years would have passed placidly, too.

Yes, he was surely all that ladies were told they should want. Of good fortune, steady temper, respectable. But if she had married such a man, she wouldn't have Marie. Wouldn't have her work and the deep fulfilment it brought. Life had such twists and turns, so different from what they were all told to expect.

But he did seem nice enough, and Sandrine needed all the friends she could find on her solitary path. 'Good evening, Lord Charlecote! Are you enjoying the assembly?'

'I am indeed, Madame Dumas. But I am sure I would enjoy it a great deal more if you might agree to dance with me?'

Sandrine thought of her daydream, floating on the dance floor with Alain. 'I think it does seem so crowded, and I fear I'm a bit too overwhelmed to dance at the moment. I think I might enjoy a turn about the room, though.'

'I should enjoy that very much, Madame Dumas. I'm afraid my dancing skills are not of the first stare!' He offered her his arm, and she slid her hand over his sleeve. He smelled quite pleasant, of soap and snow, and he was lean and handsome, all that he should be. Yet she felt sad there was no spark there, nothing like the heat she'd ever felt only for Alain.

Mary and Charles had finished their waltz, and now sipped lemonade near the fireplace. Mary waved at Sandrine when she glimpsed them, and raised her brows at Lord Charlecote's arm under Sandrine's touch. Sandrine bit her lip to keep from laughing. Her friend was always a matchmaker, just as Sandrine was always a *modiste*.

Lord Charlecote nodded at the Campbells. 'It is so nice to see dear Mrs. Campbell's newfound happiness, is it not? After all she had brought to others!'

'Very much. She and her sister have been such lovely friends to me, I'm delighted they both made such happy marriages themselves.' The St Aubins' sisters had made more than suitable matches indeed; they had found husbands who valued them for who they were, even for their business sense, and it gave her such a pang to think of it.

'It is quite enviable,' Lord Charlecote said, and Sandrine thought he sounded rather sad. 'Since I was widowed, I confess I have longed for nothing so much as domestic bliss and comfort. It is such a yearning.'

'Indeed, I understand.' She had begun to feel just such impossible yearning herself. 'It's sad we can't all be as blessed as Mary and Charles have been.'

'Exactly!' He pressed her hand. 'I could use just such a soft lady's touch in my own life.'

'I...' Sandrine, whose work so depended on finding the right words at the right moment, to be descriptive, patient, kind, now had no words. 'It is—is difficult, *oui*. I—I think I suddenly feel quite warm.'

He gave her an indulgent smile, pressed her hand again. She longed to snatch her hand away, to run into the crowd, and she hated a woman's powerlessness in that moment. 'I do know ladies are often so overcome by delicate emotions. I have surprised you, but surely you must have guessed my feelings?'

'I—no,' she said faintly.

That smile widened. 'Shall I fetch some lemonade?'

'Thank you, yes, how kind.' At last he let her go, drifted away. She watched until he vanished, and she could draw a breath again.

She backed away, waiting until she could spin around and run for the withdrawing room, but a solid weight was behind her. She bumped into something tall, warm, and twirled about to find Alain in her path.

'Sandrine!' he said with a happy smile, that smile that had lingered in her dreams for so many years. That dashing smile of his! But was it all in her imagination now, her wild hopes that something might have changed? She had been so very mistaken in him before.

His smile flickered uncertainly. 'I hoped you would be here tonight. I have been looking for you.'

And there was that excitement again, that wild hope. Had he really wanted to see her, even as she had him? 'Have you?' she said, making herself laugh. 'I think it would be hard to find even an elephant in such a crush!'

He chuckled, that deep, warm, smooth sound that made her shiver. 'Exactly. I feel like I know not a soul, since Francoise disappeared with her friend Adele, and there is nothing quite so lonely as a crowd.'

'That is true.' How often she'd felt so alone in the years without him. But she could never let him know that.

He glanced around, an empty wine glass dangling carelessly from his long fingers. 'But I thought I saw you just now with your admirer.'

'Admirer?' She could barely seem to remember anything from before Alain had appeared.

'A gentleman in a green coat. You seemed in very earnest conversation.' He frowned, and she wondered if he could possibly be jealous.

For an instant, she was rather tempted to explore that hint of jealousy, to see where it might go, but she could not play such games. Not with him. 'He is Lord Charlecote. A friend. Mary Campbell introduced us.'

He tilted his head as he watched her, trying to read her as he always could. 'I am sure you have many admirers. How could they help themselves? You look so—so...' His voice faded, as if he could not find the words. As if he was as lost as she was.

'I am not free to have—admirers,' she whispered. Yet he must have had many on his travels, just as he had in Bath. Women flocking around him in her own salon, at the theatre. Yes, she knew all too well how hard it was to resist him.

He glanced around at the crowd. 'Would you care to dance?'

Oh, yes, indeed she would! To feel his body against hers, to move as one with him, just as she had fantasised. To touch his hand, breathe in the scent of him. She longed for it so much it hurt. But she had to remember to be careful.

His head tilted again, a grin on his lips, his expression turning—was it *daring*? As if he knew her hesitant thoughts. Oh, yes, that smile was definitely mischievous now, as if he did dare her to dance with him, touch him, be close to him, with everyone watching. As if he dared her to give way to her desires, her old way of throwing herself into emotion whenever she was near him.

And she could not resist. 'Oh, very well. Just one dance. I must give all my admirers a chance, as you say.'

He laughed exuberantly, and seized her hand as if he would twirl her around and around until she was dizzy. 'But I am the foremost admirer among them, I assure you.'

He stood back and bowed properly, offering her his arm. Oh, yes, all very proper, yet there was something of a lightning *frisson* in that simple, everyday movement. She knew so well how it would feel to touch him, the awareness, *aliveness* that would sizzle over her skin. Yet she couldn't back away now. She slid her hand over his sleeve, glad she wore gloves so he could not see she still wore his sapphire ring. She'd long ago changed it to her right hand, but she couldn't let go of it entirely.

The whole room, the whole world, stilled when he touched her, everything freezing but the pounding of her heart.

He led her through the crowd towards the dance floor. She kept her head high, her smile in place, with long years of practice in hiding her feelings, of always looking cool and amused despite everything swirling beneath. It had grown so hard over the years; it was almost impossible now that time had caught up to her once again.

They found a place amid the couples, a spot for their own waltz, and Alain's hand came to her waist. Warm, strong, making her shiver. She felt her smile wobble, but a great force of will kept it in place, and she looked beyond Alain's shoulder. She saw Lord Charlecote watching them sadly, Mary with a wide-eyed amazement, Françoise looking rather satisfied before she whispered to Adele. Then the others grew blurry, and she became lost in *him*.

'We have never danced before,' he said hoarsely.

'Have we not? I cannot recall,' Sandrine answered lightly. It was not true, of course. She remembered everything. Every moment. All the excitement, the wonder. The raw need.

Perhaps they had danced together in her girlish

dreams, her old hopes. The fantasy of it felt real, as if this moment had happened before so many times.

The music began, and they swayed into motion together. At first, their steps seemed out of order, but their bodies remembered each other, remembered their rhythm, and they dipped and swayed and spun. It was dizzying, disorienting, making her world change and blur until there was only him.

He looked so very serious as he looked down at her, his hand guiding her. 'I understand, Sandrine.'

For a moment, she had to concentrate on her feet, and was distracted. But she was caught by his strange tone. 'Understand?'

'You have made a new life. Maybe found a new love.'

She stumbled. 'New love?'

'Lord Charlecote. If you want to be free, to make a new start…'

She was so shocked, she stumbled even more badly, nearly falling until he caught her. He thought she loved Lord Charlecote? That she wanted her freedom? When they twirled to the edge of the floor, she grabbed his hand and drew him with her through the crowd, her smile feeling frozen and brittle on her face. Along a corridor beyond the main staircase, she managed to find a quiet, darkened little sitting room, stacked with storage crates, the music and laughter a faint echo. She pulled him inside and shoved the door closed behind them.

They stared at each other in the hot, dark silence,

and Sandrine couldn't breathe. Her chest felt so tight, her fingers and toes numb. There, in the silvery moonlight from the window, he looked like—like magic. Like no time had passed at all. But she had to remind herself of the chasm of pain that lay between them. She had so much to lose now if she trusted him again.

'You think I want a divorce? To marry again?' she whispered.

He ran his hand through his curls. 'I know it's been a long time. I would understand, truly. It would be difficult, but if we wanted that…'

'Do *you* want that? To be free of me?'

'Sandrine. We are not speaking of me. I only want you to be happy, to help you if I can, to—to…' He broke off, shaking his head in a most adorable fashion.

Sandrine hardly knew what she was doing, couldn't control herself. She took one step, two, crossing that divide between them, reached up and seized his perfect cravat. She crumpled its fine muslin in her gloved fist, and he widened his eyes, startled. Good, now he was as off-balance as she. She pulled him to her, stretched up on her toes, and kissed him.

All the old, hot, swept-away passion of their wedding night flooded back over her, seized her, lifted her. Her body remembered, it *knew*, and so did his. He seemed to remember, too; his arms came around her, hard, his kiss deepening into hers, filled with need. Answering her hunger with hunger.

He tasted of wine and mint. He tasted of *trouble*, as though her careful life was toppling all around her and she didn't even want to stop it. It was the same as before, but so, so different. Now she knew exactly where it led.

She slid her hands over his chest, feeling the hard heat of him under the layers of wool and linen, over his powerful shoulders. They kissed as if they'd been starving for years, as if every lonely night, every regret, was torn away and there was only raw need.

She reached up and tangled her fingers in his hair, felt his hands on her back, her hips, tugging her closer and closer. She was drowning, drowning in the way he felt, the smell of him, the taste of him. She would be driven quite mad if she stayed there with him like that. Such yearning would surely destroy, leave ashes in its wake. But she had to stay a little longer, just a little longer…

'Sandrine,' he groaned, his lips sliding from hers to kiss her throat, lick at the tiny pulse that beat at its base. *'Ma belle…'*

Oh, yes, how she wanted to stay right there forever! She wanted all her old dreams back again, wanted to lose herself in him, in his strength, and be safe.

But she knew all too well what would come next. Safety with Alain was an illusion. Pain would come after the fire of passion.

She pulled away, wrenching herself out of his arms, and turned her back to the sight of him to try and recapture her control. She glimpsed her reflection in the window glass, her pale face, her hair tumbling free, and Alain behind her. He raised his hand towards her, only for it to drop away. He ran his fingers through his curls.

'Let me—let me take you home,' he whispered roughly. His hand flexed, twitched, and she longed, dreaded, for him to reach for her again. 'Sandrine...'

She couldn't bear it a moment longer. She took another step away, and another, more firmly this time. She smoothed her skirts with shaking hands. '*Non*, Alain. We can't. Not now.'

His fingers raked through his hair again, and left it on end. 'It's different now. *I* am different. Let me show you, prove it to you.'

She dared to glance back at him, to look into the stormy sea of his eyes. It didn't *feel* different. She was still wild for him, filled with longing that threatened to dash away everything else. Yet he was right. It was all so different now. She'd been a fool to forget that even for a moment.

There was Marie. And she couldn't keep Alain from her any longer. It wasn't right.

She held her hand up to keep him away, at a safer distance. 'Come tomorrow,' she said. She whispered her address before she could change her mind. 'We must talk.'

'Yes,' he answered eagerly. 'Yes, we must. I have so much to say to you, Sandrine. Just give me the chance to show you how I really have changed, to earn your trust again. However long it takes.'

Yet Sandrine knew he would no longer trust *her* once he learned the full truth.

She nodded, her throat tight with tears, and ran from the room before she could throw herself back into his arms and lose everything in his kiss all over again.

Alain sent his carriage away as he left the Assembly Rooms, unable to stay still. Françoise was staying on with the Campbells and Adele, and so he would walk back to his rented house, take in the fresh, cold air, the stars, the quiet of the city as he struggled to cool his racing thoughts—and his wildly aroused body.

He laughed at himself as he dashed down the street, past a startled couple on their way into the assembly. Years ago, he could never have imagined the emotion coursing through him now, all over his own wife! The exhilaration, hope, fear, passion. Even a year ago, in his restless wanderings, his yearning for something just beyond his touch, his understanding, he could not have known that what he longed for was right there, already in his life.

What a young fool he'd been in those far-away, heedless days. How he'd wanted dreams he couldn't have, that were not real. He could remember now the intensity of his first, young, inspired-by-epic-poetry passion for Danielle Aurac, by what her beauty, her mystery, had made him think he felt. But now, it was as if it had all happened to someone else. It felt unreal, hazy, distant, lost in all he had seen, experienced, learned since then. Why had he ever thought he'd do anything to be with her, that his feelings were worth hurting anyone over, especially Sandrine? It was unfathomable now, confusion and self-loathing left in its place. Guilt. Longing for something real now.

Something that maybe, just maybe, he could have had long ago if he hadn't been so blind.

He stopped beside the river, taking in the enfolding night all around him. The silver moonlight glittered over the roofs, turning everything pale and magical. He wished he was an artist, as Sandrine was, that he could capture in paint and keep forever the way she'd looked in her gown, there across the Assembly Room floor. She had been a pretty girl when they had met, fresh and shy, but now she'd unfurled and was utterly breathtaking. She made him think of other transcendent sights he'd glimpsed, deserts at night, Paris in the early morning with sunrise-pink over the bridges, minarets, oceans. How he wished she'd been there beside him to share it all, to see it with her artist's eye and become enraptured with its beauty as he had been. She made him see things more brightly, more clearly.

He'd felt so alone then, not sure what was really missing, what would make the beautiful world whole. Had it really been Sandrine all that time? Every moment he was with her now twined them closer. One thing seemed the same as it had been back then, one precious thing—when Sandrine looked at him, it was as if her artist's eye truly saw him, the first one who ever really did. His family, Danielle, his friends, they saw what they imagined, what they wanted him— set him—to be. Whereas Sandrine looked at him so steadily, unblinkingly, and seemed to peer down to a secret soul even he couldn't glimpse. Just as he thought he saw the true her. Once, she'd still wanted to be with him. Now...

Now he couldn't imagine why she would. Not after how he had behaved back then, and all that lay between them. She had a life here, admirers. She'd become a great beauty filled with quiet confidence, pleasure in her work, in herself. And he knew he wasn't the only one who just loved to be in her presence. Lord Charlecote, for instance, whose intentions had been clear for everyone in the Assembly Rooms to see.

And he thought of their kiss, so unexpected and glorious. He barely restrained himself from throwing back his head and howling at the moon. What should he do now? There had to be a way to show her he'd truly changed, that he was no longer that wild young man who knew nothing. He knew what he *wanted* to do: catch her up in his arms, carry her off to a bedchamber, never let her go. But what would win her heart again?

She'd pushed him away there after their kiss. If she hadn't, he would have lost himself, forgotten everything but her. But he didn't want their first time together again to be quick, heedless, but filled with the knowledge that *now* was very different from then. They were different, and he would prove that to her. No matter how great a torture it had been to give up the intoxicating feel of her body against his, the sweet taste of her.

She'd agreed to see him again. That must be a good sign. A start to the work he had to do now, the truth he must show her. Their future depended on it.

Chapter Twelve

Sandrine sat perched on one of the benches scattered amid the green near her house, watching children race past with their balls and hoops, their cloaks flying, while white-capped nannies chased after them. It was a cold but sunny day in Bath, fluffy clouds hopping by like sheep overhead, casting little shadows over the honey-coloured houses and gleaming windows, and the merry giggles and happy shouts of the children cheered and steadied her.

She needed a great deal of steadying that morning. It had been a sleepless night, tossing beneath her blankets as her mind turned over every second with Alain in their hidden closet at the assembly. That kiss, that kiss! Oh, what a mistake it had been. Yet so delicious.

Then, not content with tormenting her over her out-of-control desire for him, her mind had thrown her back to those long-ago days she'd tried so hard to forget. The moments she'd realised her marriage would not be as she had dreamed. That she'd been foolish.

At last, sure she wouldn't sleep at all, she'd got up and tiptoed across the landing to Marie's nursery.

Her daughter was fast asleep in her frilled pink and white bed, her favourite doll cuddled close, her rosebud mouth pursed in her dreams. Her tangled dark curls spilled over her pillows, and Sandrine smoothed them back.

She was sure her heart would burst with joy as she watched Marie, would burst with the force of love and worry, just as it had since the day that miraculous little creature appeared in her life, her arms. If only she could have held that tiny soul safe against her forever!

People, except maybe great poets and great artists, seemed to think a joy meant any pleasure in life. Happiness. Light. It was not so. Happiness was her work, her memories. Joy, which came by so rarely, was mingled with pain. With fear. When she had first seen Alain, she knew now that was a joy. Marie was the supreme joy. Sandrine had vowed only to protect her.

She tucked the bedclothes closer around Marie now, inhaling deeply of her sleeping-baby scent of powder and warmth. Marie was growing so fast. She asked so many questions about things she'd never been interested in before. Sandrine knew she could not delay another day, could not let fear dictate what she must do. She had to tell Alain. Her daughter deserved it.

And yes, Alain deserved it, too.

The Alain she had once known, when they were both so young—she couldn't have imagined him a father, couldn't imagine him standing still long enough, focusing long enough on something so precious. She had tried to find him back then, to tell him she'd discovered she was pregnant, but in strictest truth she'd not tried quite as hard as she should have. It was that fear that had stayed her hand. The fear he would hurt her again. Much worse, that he might hurt their daughter. Might reject her as he had rejected Sandrine.

The Alain she saw now, though...he was different. She saw the experience in his eyes, the solemnity, the calm core he'd found. This was a secret she could not keep now. *Secret* seemed too small a word for it all. She had to conquer her fear.

She closed her eyes and tipped back her head to let a hint of the day's pale sunlight wash over her face, hoping that light might fortify her. If only it weren't quite so early in the day for a large brandy...

'Sandrine,' she heard a voice say. A voice she would have known anywhere, even in those years they'd spent apart, Orpheus-like, calling her to him from the darkness.

She opened her eyes and blinked up at Alain. The light surrounded him like a halo, outlining the sharp angles of his face, the tentative smile on his lips. She studied those lips, remembering every instant of their kiss last night, every sensation of it.

'Alain,' she whispered. 'Thank you for meeting me here. You got my note?'

'Of course. I was glad to see it,' he said, and sat down beside her. They did not touch, but he crossed one booted foot over his knee and rested his gloved hand there lightly, so close to her. The chilly breeze caught his delicious scent, and wrapped it around her as tightly as any rope bonds. 'I was rather worried it would mean...' He broke off, and ran his hand through his curls in that adorable gesture she remembered too well.

'Worried?' she said. She dared not look at him directly, not let her guard down.

'That I tried to push you too far last night, that I—well, pressured you too much?' He seemed a bit ruffled, a bit unsure, and it made her heart ache even more. 'Just being with you, feeling you. It had been so long, and I think you are...' The hand through the hair again, leaving it ruffled. 'I think you are amazing. Just as I remembered.'

He had thought of her in the years they were parted? Remembered their brief union? She hoped that meant he cherished a bit of tenderness in his memories, and would forgive her once he knew. She gathered up all her courage, more than it even took to love and still go into the world on her own, to open her shop, to do anything else at all, and said, 'Alain. I must tell you something very important indeed.'

He studied her closely, making her twist her hands nervously in her lap. 'So I did go too far. Maybe you are in love with Charlecote?'

Sandrine was shocked. Love was the furthest thing from her thoughts. 'In love with—anyone? Certainly not. I have never thought myself in love at all.' Except once, with Alain himself. And that had been a great mistake.

'Then what? You can tell me anything at all. I know

you may not believe it yet, but I will prove you can trust me again.'

She laughed nervously. 'You are not making this easy, watching me so intently.' It was as if he tried to read her thoughts again, read her inner heart, no matter how she tried to conceal it.

He looked away. 'Sorry.'

A silence fell between them, delicate, ephemeral, like a shimmering soap bubble and as easy to break.

'Sandrine,' he said finally. 'You really can trust me with anything. Let me prove that to you, to try and show you. I know it is hard for you to believe—perhaps impossible, after all we've been through—but I really have changed.'

She nodded. But could she, dared she, give him that chance? Look what had happened last time. She studied him from the corner of her eyes, found that he watched her, leaned towards her. She read nothing but sincerity on his face.

'I know you may not, cannot believe me yet,' he said quietly. 'I behaved so badly. If what you wish now is to find a way to end our marriage...'

She was startled by him again. 'End it?'

'Is that not what you want to talk about today? I know it would be very difficult, but I want to see you happy...'

She had to laugh. 'After our kiss? How could you think it?'

He frowned in puzzlement. 'That kiss was—*etonnante*. But what else can I think, after so long? You deserve to have whatever you want in life, Sandrine. I owe you that, and so much more.'

And he, too, deserved happiness, deserved his dreams. Maybe he really did still love Danielle, or someone like her. But more than that, he deserved to *know*. 'This is what I want to tell you, Alain. Let me say it fast, before I lose my courage.'

She reached quickly into her reticule, before she really did lose her courage and resolve, and drew out the pearl-edged case of the miniature portrait she'd tucked there. She reached for his hand, and he gave it to her. She longed to clutch at his strength, to hold on, even though it could easily shatter everything for her now. She pressed the ivory into his palm and prayed he couldn't hear the fearful hammering of her heart.

He turned it over, staring down at it with a thoughtful crease between his dark brows. The moment felt like an hour, like an eternity. She'd imagined it so often over the years, and her images had involved shouting, demands, even embraces. This was just silence.

Sandrine rather hoped that Marie's dark curls, a wild halo around her little heart-shaped face, her grey-blue eyes and stubborn chin, would tell Alain all he needed to know and she wouldn't have to find the words. Her throat was too dry, her cheeks hot. But the silence grew longer, heavier, as if it would push her down into the earth.

At last he looked up at her, his beautiful face as smooth and unreadable as marble. *'Qu'est-ce que c'est?'*

Sandrine drew in a long, deep breath, wishing that one long sip of cold air could go on forever. 'That is Marie. My daughter.' *Our daughter.* Alain watched her, unblinking, unwavering. 'She is nearly five.'

His study went back to the portrait. 'She is beautiful,' he said quietly. She could read nothing in his tone, the blank lines of his face.

A terrible thought landed on Sandrine, one she should have considered before but which she had not in her fear of his reaction. Maybe he thought Marie was the child of another man. 'Very beautiful. Her eyes...' His eyes. Marie also had his spirit of adventure, his stubbornness, his way of leaping into something and thinking about it later. She had his tenderness.

'And what you are saying, I assume, is that she is my child.'

Sandrine couldn't talk at all; she choked on every word she thought of. So many moments over the years she'd been alone in the world washed over her. The fear when she'd first found out she was pregnant, the uncertainty of her next step. 'Yes.'

His fingers curled tightly around the pearl edges of the frame. 'Oh, Sandrine,' was all he said.

What could she read into those two words? Was he angry, sad, regretful, scared? She took another breath, and plunged ahead. There could be no going back now.

'It happened, of course, on our wedding night. Our silly, strange wedding night. I was so foolish, so young, I didn't realise until a long time later. You had left on your travels, and I knew you deserved your freedom after all that had happened. I knew—well, I knew of your feelings for Mademoiselle Aurac. I just didn't know what to do.'

Alain did not shout at her, berate her. He didn't demand things. He didn't even look at her. His boots dropped to the ground, and he leaned on his knees, staring at the painting in his hand. 'Tell me more,' was all he said.

Oh, there was so much more to tell him! Marie's first little steps, her first words, her favourite doll, her favourite stories, her silly little-child jokes. Sandrine didn't know what he wanted, where to start. 'I went away to a little village near the sea, found a nurse. I didn't dare tell our families. And when she was born, she was so very small. She was a bit early, you see. The midwife wasn't sure she would even live.'

And Sandrine had thought it a punishment for the mess she'd made of her marriage. She'd been scared, hadn't wanted a child. When she looked into that tiny face, after all those hours of pain, she'd been flooded with love and longing. Just like when she had first seen Alain, and she'd known that somehow everything would change.

'But I knew,' she went on, 'when I held her, she would live and be strong, a little warrior. My Joan of Arc! How she would shout and wave her tiny fists all night and day. I thought she was like you. Stubborn, sure of herself.'

So Marie had turned out to be. Stubborn, passionate, sweet and loving. 'We have such fun together!

She loves to sing and laugh, tell stories, make her little drawings. She is my gift. I never, ever should have kept her from you. I should have tried so much harder to tell you, I know that. But if there was a chance for you, a chance for you and Mademoiselle Aurac to be together...'

She wasn't sure now what she thought then, what was up and what was down. Exhausted by the memories, by her old fears, she slumped back against the bench, shaking with emotion. With that weakness, there was also a strange relief. Alain knew everything at last. Whatever was meant to happen could now be set free. She could put down that weight of fear and guilt she'd carried for so long.

'Maudire, Sandrine!' Alain suddenly snapped. His fist tightened around the portrait, and he shook his head. 'I have a *daughter*. Why did you not tell me the instant we met again?'

'I—I was scared,' was all she could say. She started to reach for him, and her hand dropped again. That fear was still there. 'And I promised her when she was born I would always protect her. I just didn't always know how best to do that.'

He sucked in a deep breath, and his head dropped, everything going still and calm. 'I see. Yes.'

Sandrine had the wildest hope. 'Do you?'

'Of course. You say you were young and foolish when we wed. So was I, a thousand times more so. I had such ideas, such wild notions! I wasn't able to see then what I had, what the future could be. What my commitments truly were. I cannot say now what that boy might have done, had he known. But I am not him now. Not entirely.' He turned his head to look at her, and she shivered with the raw pain on his face, the emotions roiling in his eyes. 'I have seen so much, learned so much. But I promise, Sandrine, I am not scared now. I see what I have.' He laughed ruefully. 'Well, not *entirely* scared.'

Sandrine dared venture a joke. 'Marie is certainly very fearsome, I agree.'

'Is she?' he asked eagerly. 'I want to know! I want to know so many things, everything.' He slid closer to her on the bench, watching her with such a force of hope in his eyes it made her ache. 'Can we at last find a way to trust each other?'

She studied him in return, taking in every shift of his expression, every movement. How she longed for that, longed to know things had truly changed. 'I think we must.'

He nodded. 'Then may I meet her? Meet Marie?'

'Yes.' She had to force away that fear in the hopes of moving at last into full, bright light. It was the hardest thing she'd ever done. She'd worked so hard to build this life with Marie, to protect her daughter, to protect her own heart. She could see Alain was not the same man he'd been when they first met, just as she was not the same idealistic girl. But would she regret letting him in? The problem was, she knew she had no choice. She needed to do this. For him and for Marie. For the opportunity for them to know one another. To love one another. So she had to take the chance and leap, and hope her safeguards were enough.

Alain was sure this couldn't be real. He was walking through a dream, a haze. A second before and after that seemed to divide the whole world.

He had a child. He had a wife and daughter. He had let them down in terrible ways. He could not do that again.

But, blast it all! How could he have prevented it? How could he have known *he* was what they needed?

He glanced at Sandrine as they walked along the street, as she talked to him about their daughter. She looked so calm, so closed-in upon herself, though her face was pale beneath her stylish little hat. Since he found her again, he'd marvelled at her beauty and strength, her talent, all she had accomplished. Now he realised he hadn't seen even a fraction of her real strength. Had *she* changed, or was it just the way he had changed himself, how he saw the world now?

She looked up at him, her eyes wide. She looked so scared, as he felt, but also brave. She had clearly decided on something, resolved to trust him with the most precious thing in the world. He couldn't let her down.

'... She adores marzipan, and won't always eat her vegetables,' Sandrine was saying, continuing to tell him every titbit about Marie, and every morsel he eagerly consumed. 'And when she visits the seaside, she eats mussels by the dozen! So French, I think.'

As they neared Sandrine's house, their steps slowed.

'Sandrine,' Alain said. 'When she was born—what did you tell people? How did your family behave?'

She laughed, and he wondered if that was a good sign, if things had not been as difficult as he feared. 'My parents were quite happy! A child that might be a *comte* one day, though of course she turned out to be a girl. Before my father died, he quite doted on her when we saw them, which was not often because of my work. And when I learned how to run my business, I told people, told Marie, that you travelled a great deal and we would see you when your business permitted, and I had to keep myself busy with my gowns. It has been a hard life, but Bath is a nice place for a child, with so many parks and amusements.'

He turned her words over in his mind, aching at all he had missed. All *they* had missed.

Sandrine bit her lip, as if uncertain about his silence. 'As I said, I tried to write to you, Alain, once I knew. You were gone on your travels by then, and I always feared my letters went astray, or that you...' She shook her head, and he was afraid he knew what her next words would be.

'You thought I would not care,' he said quietly. 'Oh, Sandrine. I never meant to stay away so long. It's just... There was always another business deal in the next city, the next challenge I wanted to meet. I had so longed to prove myself, to know I could make my own way in the world.'

'And so did I! Look at what we have both accomplished,' she said, pressing his hand in hers. 'I know that neither of us meant for things to happen in quite this way. We both needed our work, needed to prove ourselves. Soon I was so busy with Marie and my work, I suppose I knew we would meet again somehow, and then...' She laughed again, ruefully. 'I don't know, really.'

'It could not have been easy, raising her on your own, running your shop.'

'Not always, no,' she whispered, and he found he longed to know everything that happened to her, everything she saw, every challenge she faced, so he could make it easier. Make it all up to her. 'Especially when she was an infant, I had no idea what I was doing! I tried to change nappies and fastened them the wrong way. She would give me such a disdainful look.'

Alain laughed to imagine his elegant wife handling nappies. She laughed, too, and it was a wonderful, warm moment shared between them, as if they had watched it together. Learned together. 'I was lonely at times,' she said. 'Afraid our lives could not work out as I hoped. But I learned. You will, too.'

He laid his other hand atop hers, marvelling at the strength in its daintiness. 'Sandrine. How I wish I had been there for you, always. I—I regret so many things. I want to know everything I missed! First words, first steps, things she hates. Does she like peas? I never did. I just... Everything. If you will let me.'

She smiled softly. 'Alain. Perhaps you should just begin by meeting her.'

He nodded, feeling silly, eager, so young and uncertain again. 'Shall I tell her who I am?'

'Soon, I think. She does think you have been travelling, working for us, buying and selling beautiful things. We look at atlases sometimes, wondering where you are, what you have seen. She does love tales of adventure! I know she must know very soon. You deserve that, both of you. But let us take one careful step at a time.'

He knew she was right. This was too precious, too important, to ruin now. He had to build new relationships slowly, carefully. 'Yes. I shall do as you say.'

She gestured towards the house just ahead. 'Let's make a start, then.'

They reached the front steps of a house, a small, calm, respectable-looking town house inscrutable behind its draperies, its polished front steps. He looked up at it, at the serenely gleaming windows that concealed so much, and felt her hand alight on his arm. Holding them both steady.

'Do you want to go inside?' she asked quietly.

'Of course I do.' But he hesitated on the first stone step. He had to tell her, assure her, even though he knew it would be a long road to that. 'I was not there when you most needed me, Sandrine, but I want to be there now.'

Did she believe him? He couldn't tell, not from the steadiness with which she studied him. She just opened the door.

She led him into a small hallway, a staircase winding above, a few doors opening into sitting rooms, dining rooms, paintings on the walls, a soft, faded carpet underfoot. He remembered her parents' grand London home, and his parents' shabby dwelling there, the sense he'd always had of never being really at home. Sandrine had created a very homely space, one all her own, filled with artistry. The soft, welcoming blues and pale yellows created a haven of comfort, of rest.

'*Madame,*' a maidservant greeted them, studying Alain curiously.

'*Bonjour, Julie.*' Sandrine handed her the reticule, her hat and gloves, and gestured for Alain to take off his greatcoat. 'Have Mademoiselle Sophie and Marie returned yet?'

'*Oui, madame,* just now. I have sent up some cocoa to the nursery. Shall I call for them?'

'No, don't rush them. Could we have some tea in the drawing room?'

She turned, and led him into a small room, as elegant as everything else she touched with yellow and springtime blue, stacks of books, open workboxes, paintings in gilded frames. Quite nervous, he found he couldn't stand still, and wandered the perimeter of the pink and blue floral carpet to study the paintings on the blue-papered walls, the books on the shelves. French novels, poetry, art.

Sandrine sat down carefully on the edge of a blue and white striped settee, watching him warily.

'You have made yourself a beautiful home,' he said. 'It feels so full of—of comfort and welcome.'

She laughed, and gestured to the stacks of books, the workboxes overflowing with ribbons. 'You mean a mess?'

'Not at all! I mean, it is yours, it could belong to no one else. It speaks of you. Of your elegance and beauty, your spirit that draws people in. Makes them feel seen.'

She looked away, her cheeks growing dark pink. She took up a cushion and fiddled with its tassels. 'I fear I am the despair of my maids. Marie is allowed in any room, and she does tend to leave her dolls and toys around.' She nudged at some blocks with the toe of her half-boot.

'It's not much like my parents' house was,' he murmured as he examined a cluster of framed miniatures on the fireplace mantel. 'The *comte* and *comtesse* would never allow anything from the nursery into a drawing room.'

'But *you* are the *comte* now,' she said quietly.

'So I am. But I don't like to think about any of that.' It was really that title, that useless old French title, that had brought them where they were. Sandrine's father's purchasing of it, his parents' driving need to preserve it.

Sandrine seemed to think of that as well. She frowned down at the cushion. 'Titles are only what we make of them.'

He nodded, remembering that she had said she wanted a Parisian shop of her own. 'Surely being a *comtesse* could help you if you opened a business in France.'

She tilted her head back to study him, her eyes narrowed. 'I suppose it could, yes.'

'So I could help you in that small way?' At last there was something useful he could do for her!

She shook her head. 'Alain. You don't have to do anything for me.'

'But I do. I want to. Surely I owe you that?' And so much more. He took a step towards her, longing to take her hand, to be next to her, but something held him back.

He could see she wanted to protest, but there was an echo of running feet on the staircase, the drawing room door pushed open. Sandrine rose to her feet, a wide smile spreading over her whole face, lighting up her eyes. She looked as radiant as a summer's day.

'Maman, Maman!' A tiny, curly-haired whirlwind flew into the room and threw her arms around Sandrine's waist. Her pink hair ribbon was quite undone, ends trailing from those dusky curls, and her white skirt hem was dusty above little kid boots. Her plump cheeks glowed pink. Yet no spirit of mischief could disguise her rare, perfect beauty, her long neck and heart-shaped face, her dark blue eyes that were all d'Alency.

He could not breathe, could not move. Everything sharpened, intensified. His whole life felt it had come down to just this one second.

'Mademoiselle Sophie took me to Sydney Gardens!' she piped, her accent touched at the edges with the air of France. She was oblivious to his presence, which Alain was glad of. It gave him time to collect himself, to not frighten Marie with the intensity of his reaction. 'We played with hoops! Can we go to Mollands this afternoon? I love it so! I was very, very good, I promise. I listened to Mademoiselle Sophie very carefully, and minded her.'

Sandrine held her close, protective as she studied Alain over Marie's ruffled head. Her eyes were wide, wary. 'Yes, we can go to Mollands very soon and get you some marzipan. But right now we have a guest.'

Marie spun around to stare at him with a surprised, curious stare. Her eyes were large, dark blue, as bright as a night star. It made him think of his mother, his sisters. The eyes he saw in the mirror every day.

Everything else in the world faded, vanished. He hardly noticed the maid coming in with the tea tray, didn't hear the clatter of the silver and porcelain, didn't hear Sandrine's murmured instructions. He didn't know what to say, what to do, he'd never been so nervous and speechless before.

Sandrine took her daughter's little hand, and Marie drew back against her skirts. 'Marie, *chère*, this is Monsieur le Comte d'Alency. Will you say *bonjour*?'

Marie blinked up at him, studying him most carefully, just as Sandrine did. He found he couldn't stop studying her, either. He wanted to memorise every detail, fill every moment he'd missed. She was so beautiful.

Marie tiptoed forward and bobbed an admirable little curtsey, despite her wide, astonished eyes. '*Bonjour, Monsieur le Comte.* I am Mademoiselle Marie Dumas.'

'I am most pleased indeed to meet you, Mademoiselle Marie.' He bowed low to her, making her giggle, the most musical little sound. *'Comment allez-vous?'*

She laughed again, and it made her look just like her mother when she was delighted by something. It gave Alain a deep warm glow to see it. 'Is a *comte* like a prince? I love my books about Cendrillon, but you do not look much like the paintings in them.'

He leaned close and said confidingly, 'Do not tell the princes you know, but it is better.'

She looked quite delighted. 'I want to know all about *comtes*, then! Do you have a castle?'

'We should let our guest have his tea, Marie,' Sandrine said.

Marie seized his hand in her small fingers, shocking him, flooding him with a new, rare, burning joy. 'Shall us sit and talk, then?' she said, tugging him towards the settee, as dignified as any dowager duchess.

'I should love nothing better, *mademoiselle*,' he answered in awe. He perched on the edge of the settee with her, and glanced at Sandrine to find her looking worried. He was filled with nothing but longing then, yearning to prove to her he could be trusted now, that he could hold on to this rare feeling forever and never let it slip away again. She and Marie were all he wanted now.

Chapter Thirteen

'Will you take her away?' Sandrine had strictly forbidden herself from asking Alain that, would not let the heavy worries that kept her up at night show to him. She had the upper hand, she'd told herself, but she knew that wasn't true. Alain was the man, the *comte*; they were married. He could do what he chose.

The man she'd married, that she'd fallen for in such dizzying distraction, so young and careless and so headlong-romantic it made him giddily selfish—*that* man she would not have asked such a question. Years had taught her that. He still *looked* like that young man, as though no time had passed except to make him even more beautiful—until she looked into his eyes.

She saw caution now, hope, a careful slowness that was new. As they walked towards the Pump Room the day after he had met Marie, morning sunlight shining around them in a greyish-gold haze, she felt the familiar world of Bath was shaken up, turned upside-down.

He stopped short, staring down at her. For a moment she saw anger there, a shadow across his grey-blue eyes under the brim of his hat. Had she somehow hit on the terrible truth? Now that he had seen Marie, he wanted her?

What did she really know about his life now? About his dreams?

'Blast it, Sandrine,' he muttered. He walked on, making her scurry to catch up, trying to smile at the people who passed by, to not let her fear show. 'I would never do such a thing. I want to know Marie more. I want to know *everything*. But I would do nothing to hurt her or you. Please, please, do not fear me. I couldn't bear it.'

'I do not fear you,' she said carefully, and she realised she did not. Not him, but what he represented. The old life where she had been so helpless. 'Yet we both know the power here is yours. I am your wife; she is your child. I should have worked harder to tell you before. I was wrong.'

'*Non*, Sandrine. I was wrong.' He kicked at a cobblestone in his path. 'Wrong and foolish to let you go. I held a pearl, and I tossed it away when I was too young to begin to know its worth.'

Sandrine was struck speechless by those words, by the emotion that emanated from him in waves, crashing over them. 'We were both young; our families tossed us together,' she ventured. 'You loved someone else…'

He stopped short, making her bump into him. 'Love? I was infatuated with Danielle, yes, with her beauty, her mysterious ways. I imagined so many things in her.

But I've seen so much since then, learned so much. I realise now what love is. It is understanding, kindness, comfort as well as passion.'

'I should love to see such things that made you believe that,' she whispered, wondering what she might have learned at his side.

'And how much more beautiful, more profound it all would have been if you were there,' he said fiercely. He stared at her so intently she remembered their kiss at the assembly, the fire and force of it, and she couldn't breathe.

'I would give you everything, everything, Sandrine, if you would let me,' he said roughly.

Sandrine blinked away hot tears as she studied him. When she was young, when she had longed only to be with him, that was all she could have wanted. How did she feel now? Was it all too late? She felt so dizzy with it all, she hardly knew. 'Alain...'

'You said you'd like to expand your business to Paris,' he went on. 'I could help you with that. Help you and Marie make a life in Paris, I've made contacts there. If that's what you want.' He shook his head ruefully. 'I know I could not tempt you with diamonds and fine carriages. But what of art? Beauty? Just let me try. Give me some time. I would never hurt you again, never take anything from you at all.'

The crowd making their way to the Pump Room pressed around them, jostling them, and she knew they would have to move. She would have to unroot herself from the spot where she felt frozen, but she barely realised where she was. That she was still in the real world, in that cold Bath morning. 'Time. Yes. Once it was all I longed for, Alain, time with you. The girl I was then...'

'Then I give it to you now, all you want. Just let me spend more moments with you and Marie, and you will see.'

Sandrine studied his face. As she took in his unwavering gaze, she dared to let a tiny ray of hope sneak past her armour. Could she trust him? Could this be the first new step? She nodded, and took his outstretched arm to let him lead her inside. After the chill outside, the room was warm and crowded, bright, swirling, with the clink of glasses, the strains of the string quartet playing.

'Sandrine!' she heard Mary Campbell call to her, and saw her friend hurrying through the crowd lining up to peruse the arrivals book, get their vile glasses of water. But Mary looked like summer sunshine itself in her Madame Dumas gown and spencer of pale yellow and white. With her was Françoise. 'My dear, we were just talking of you.'

Sandrine made herself smile, and kissed Mary lightly on both cheeks. 'Should I be nervous, *amie*?'

'Never!' Mary declared with a laugh. 'You are the most fascinating lady in Bath, as well as a darling friend. Of course we must speak of you.' She glanced at Alain, her eyes wide with curiosity. 'And you must be Françoise's handsome brother.'

Sandrine quickly made the introductions, trying not

to give her own emotions about Alain away, trying to pretend he was a mere new acquaintance.

'I told Madame Campbell I am so hoping you will take me as a new client, and I am sure I need a walking dress just like hers. That jonquil colour, so heavenly!' Françoise said as she joined them. 'Your gowns are surely the stuff of legend.'

Sandrine laughed, delightfully distracted from Alain and the great puzzle of him. 'Legend? *Mon Dieu!* I must charge more, then.'

'They say any bride who wears one of your creations is destined for great happiness,' Françoise added.

'Just look at me, and my sister Ella,' Mary said. 'Blissfully happy!'

'So I know I must have one… I can't take "maybe" for an answer.' Françoise took Sandrine's arm and pulled her into the room, Mary following with Alain until they were lost to sight among the feathered bonnets. 'And tell me, how are matters with my brother? Have you forgiven him for his idiocy? Catherine and I always did hope so much you could find a way to be happy.'

Sandrine wondered what his family really knew, what she should say. 'Did he tell you…?'

'Oh, no! Not details, of course. We were young, but not nearly as silly as our parents imagined. We saw how he behaved with his schoolmaster's granddaughter, and how she was never worthy of him at all.' She glanced around the room. 'But he has surely been served his just desserts, as it is clear that you do not need him! Your business flourishes, and look how many ladies long for your favour.'

'No. I do not *need* him.' And she was fortunate in that. She'd had seed money, had her own talents. Too many women in unhappy situations were caught, trapped. But oh, how she had once *wanted* him! He had haunted her for so long. In truth, she wanted him now, yearned for him. She glanced at him, fully aware at every moment of him, every detail of him.

'Then you must make him work very hard to deserve you,' Françoise said with a laugh. 'My dear brother has had everything too easy, I fear, with that godlike face of his, that charm. It's quite infuriating.'

Sandrine smiled to remember that was just what she'd always thought of Alain and his face—god-like, golden. But Françoise was wrong that Alain had never worked for anything, sacrificed anything. He'd sacrificed some things for his family when he married Sandrine. He'd left Sandrine to build her own life as she chose, not chasing her down, locking her away, as would have been his right. He had travelled, seen things, thought about things deeply.

He'd grown, just as she had. Could it be time for them now, as it had not been then?

As Françoise turned to speak to someone, one of Sandrine's best customers came to greet her.

'Madame Smythe!' Sandrine said. 'How lovely to see you again…it has been too long. I hope you have not been unhappy with your newest gowns?'

'Madame Dumas! How could I ever be? They are

exquisite, and make me feel ten years younger to wear them,' Mrs Smythe cried, gesturing to her dark blue pelisse *à la militaire* that had been Sandrine's work. 'I have merely been away from Bath. My poor Evelyn! What a sad thing it has been.'

'Your daughter?' Sandrine said, alarmed. She remembered Evelyn's wedding last year. Sandrine had made the mother's gown, but not the bride's, for young Evelyn insisted on more bows and swags than Sandrine could bear to feature in her work. But Evelyn had been a sweet girl, if one with rather overblown taste. 'What is amiss? Is she ill?'

Mrs Smythe sadly shook her head. 'Only in her heart. You do remember she wed last year, I am sure.'

'Of course.'

'How we were all deceived. Mr Collinsworth turned out to be quite the rake, gambling and seeking out women of light virtue at every turn; he could never let his old ways go. It is one thing to be a bit wild in a man's youth, yes, it's to be expected. But once he is older, once he marries and sets up a home, he should have purged much of that from his system. Indeed, we were sure he had. But it was not so. He quite abandoned my darling Evelyn.'

'Oh, my dear Madame,' Sandrine murmured. Maybe rakes couldn't change? But surely Alain had. She had to believe that! 'I am so very sorry.'

Mrs Smythe sighed deeply. 'I am sure I can count on your discretion.'

'Most certainly.' Secrets were as much a *modiste*'s

stock-in-trade as ribbons and lace. She'd heard shocking gossip nearly every week in her salon, and not a breath of it left her. Especially not her own scandal.

'I suppose the lesson is that a leopard never truly changes its spots. If only I could have persuaded Evelyn to commission her gown from you! She needed all the good fortune she could get.'

'Don't we all?' Sandrine murmured. Especially when it came to men with a past. But she knew what was the right thing to do now. They had to tell Marie the truth. She had to take a deep breath, leap, and trust Alain would be there. No matter how hard it would be. She glanced up and found him watching her across the room, a puzzled, concerned look on his face. She smiled, and held up her hand to indicate she was well.

'And so you are my *papa*?' Marie studied Alain's face carefully, closely. She was a most matter-of-fact child, taking the astonishing news they had just told her in her stride. She made him think of his sisters in that way.

He glanced up at Sandrine, who gave him a little nod. He had not been at all sure when she said it was time, but he had promised to follow her lead. Now it seemed she had been right, and he had to seize this moment. 'Yes, I am,' he managed to say around the lump in his throat. 'I never meant to stay away from you so long, *ma petite*.'

She nodded solemnly, the pink ribbon in her curls

bobbing. 'You had a great deal of important work to do, in very faraway places.'

'So I had, yes. But I will not leave you again. I shall do all the things *papas* do.'

She tilted her head as she studied him, frowning. 'Such as what?'

'Er...' He tried to think. His own father had seldom seen him at all before Alain was twelve or older, and his work never brought him into the orbit of families.

'Play in the gardens with your hoop,' Sandrine prompted.

'Yes!' Alain agreed eagerly. 'We shall play in the gardens, and float boats on the river. Go to Mollands for marzipan, if you like. Whatever you want.' And someday, he supposed, he would have to examine possible suitors and do things of that sort, which made him long to scoop her up and hide her away protectively! But, as Sandrine had said, one step at a time.

'I do like marzipan. Maybe you will tell me about the places you've been? We've looked at some on the maps.'

That he could do. 'I certainly will. And show you some beautiful objects from all over the world.'

'And I will have brothers and sisters, as my friends do?' Marie said.

Alain felt his face grow hot, and he dared a glance at Sandrine. Her cheeks were quite pink as well, and images flashed through his mind of their wedding night, the way her kisses tasted of honey and champagne, the sweetness of her perfume, the way they moved together so perfectly. If he could only taste that again, feel that way again...

But there were fears now, as well. If their hearts became involved, if all fell apart so painfully all over again, it would not just be the two of them hurt. It would be Marie now. He looked down at her, a tenderness and protectiveness like none he'd ever known flooding over him. He had to protect her above all.

Sandrine seemed to feel the same, as she turned to swipe at her eyes before briskly clapping her hands and smiling brightly at their daughter. 'Marie, *chérie*, why don't you run upstairs and let Mademoiselle change your frock? We must go and meet someone.'

Marie jumped up, laughing. 'Who is it now, Maman? I can't wait!'

'It is your auntie, my sister,' Alain said. He thought of how he'd told Françoise the news last night, her astonishment, her nervousness, her teasing. *You, a papa, Alain? I cannot wait to see this! Do you think she will like me?* 'Your *maman* is making her wedding gown.'

Marie twirled around, and Alain was sure Françoise needed have no fears her niece would like her. Marie had the same exuberance and delight in surprises that Françoise possessed herself. 'I have an *auntie*? And a new gown, too? I do love being with Maman while she works; she lets me help with the ribbons.'

She dashed towards the stairs, still laughing, and Alain ducked his head for a moment. He was afraid he might start crying, overwhelmed by how much things had changed in only a few moments. Sandrine seemed to understand; she moved away, nervously smoothing her gown before she gathered up a pile of sketches from a desk. Alain collected himself and put on his usual careless smile.

'Are those the sketches for Françoise's gown?' he asked.

'Yes. I do hope she likes them. I thought she might enjoy this hem…see, it makes me think of the waves of the sea. She's rather like a lovely mermaid, isn't she, with that bright hair and the way she laughs, how delightful she finds everything? Rather like Marie.'

'Yes, I thought the same thing. How much Marie is like my sisters.' He came to stand next to her, studying the images. He knew little of ladies' gowns, except when one looked inexplicably lovely on one lady and horrid on another, but he knew Sandrine knew the magic of how that worked. He could see these gowns were like no others he'd seen at theatres or balls or gardens—they were extraordinary. They seemed to speak of their own tales, their own worlds. Mermaids, yes, and forest-fairies as he'd once thought of Sandrine. Goddesses and empresses.

She seemed to be nervous at his silence, his awestruck quiet at the sight of what she could do. This was not simple dressmaking, as so many dismissed it. It was art.

'I—I thought she might like this neckline, the way it swoops just here. It's unusual, I know, but I think it would suit her quite well. She has such a bright spirit, like quicksilver. I wonder if she might even like this silver silk I found last year? I bought a bolt even though I didn't know what to do with it.' She showed him a length of shimmering, silvery-blue cloth, like something he himself would have been enticed by in an Eastern souk. She was right, it was like a mermaid, like his sister. 'It's just been waiting for the right creation. But if you think she would not like this...'

'She will love it,' he said quietly. 'How could she not? You will make her look like magic. Your work—it's astounding.'

She laughed nervously. 'I hope I am good at it by now. I've worked on it so much!'

'No, I mean—it's like nothing else I've seen.' He thought of the parcel he'd brought with him, had carried with him so long, never sure when, or if, he could give it to her. 'I have something for you.'

Her eyes widened in surprise. 'For me?'

'Wait here.' He hurried across the room to where his valise sat on a table and took out a small, paper-wrapped parcel.

Sandrine watched him, curious. He handed her the package, and the look on his face was fascinating, a blend of adorable boyish shyness, uncertainty, pride. She weighed it in her hand, wondering what it could be.

'It isn't much,' he said. 'But I saw them in a tiny shop in Marrakech, and I thought of you. Of the way you once spoke about art, about colour and movement and seeing the world in new ways.'

She smiled, remembering that conversation in the

conservatory when they had first met. It felt so long ago, but so close now, too. She unwrapped it, and found an array of powdered pigments tied up in cheesecloth bundles. Blues like deep sapphires and pale skies, butter yellow, crimson and scarlet, grass-green. So vivid they glowed.

'They are so beautiful,' she gasped.

He smiled in relief. As if she would not have liked them! 'The man in the shop said the colours are especially prized for painting tiles for mosques. They are made with rare dyes, very precious. Perhaps you could use them on silks as well!'

She studied him. She thought she might see hope there, hope like that which she held deep in her own secret heart. Hope as in *maybe* and *what if*...?

'You were far away, yet you thought of me?'

'How could I not? Oh, Sandrine. I so often heard your words when I saw a glorious sunset, or the light on ocean waves, and I wished...' He broke off, a rueful smile on his lips.

'Wished what?' she whispered.

'That you could see it, too. That I could hear what you thought of its beauty. Maybe you can use these to bring a bit of it to life.'

Sandrine held the parcel close, afraid she might start crying with longing. 'I will.'

Marie called to them, and she could say no more. But just knowing that even when they were apart he had remembered her, thought of her work, made her feel lighter.

Chapter Fourteen

'This is the house,' Alain said, pointing ahead to the rented place he must share with his sister. Sandrine studied it, suddenly quite nervous. It wouldn't just be her and Marie any more, not even just her and Marie and Alain. With Françoise, the wider world would begin to know, begin to see the little family she'd worked so hard to keep safe. What if it all went wrong?

Yet it did not *feel* wrong. The walk had been a delight, with Marie skipping along beside Alain as he told her stories of his travels. She swung his hand between them, peppering him with questions, chatty and accepting as if nothing had changed. That walk, in fact, had been been filled with some of the most wonderful moments she could ever remember. The three of them together in the sun, Marie's giggle like music on the breeze.

Sandrine thought of his gift, the brilliant pigments he'd seen in a faraway market and thought of her. He'd looked at her sketches, marvelling at them, understanding them and what they meant to her, what they meant to the ladies she wanted to help, the world she wanted to make. He'd *seen* her. And in that moment of closeness, of memory, tested by distance, the past melted away, leaving only a quiet, unspoken possible promise. He hadn't forgotten her when they were apart!

Yet there was fear, too. So much had changed in that time. So much more was at stake. She had to step very carefully.

'Will you have that tiger there in the garden?' Marie asked, twirling towards the stone front steps. 'The one you saw in India?'

Alain laughed, and Sandrine heard there the echo of the young, carefree man she'd once met in a ballroom and fallen headlong for. 'I fear he could not come to live with me... I only glimpsed him.'

'In the jungle?' Marie squealed.

'Yes. Where the air is warm and damp, and smells like spices.'

'Would I like it there?'

He studied her closely, as if evaluating. 'I am not sure. Could you ride on elephants? Carry packs through the forest?'

'Yes!' Marie cried. 'Well, a small one anyway. But I am *sure* I could ride an elephant.'

Sandrine laughed, suddenly filled with such sparkling delight as she watched the two of them together, Marie's small hand in Alain's. Their two dark heads, so similar. Tenderness washed over her, held her softly in its grip. It was delicate, not burning with passion or trembling with desire, but steady, warm, and deeply devoted. Terrifying.

Marie didn't seem to have any such fear. She dashed into the house with Alain, Sandrine trailing behind them. It was not a large hallway, but warm and inviting, filled with the scent of flowers. A carpet in glowing jewel colours spread under their feet, obviously brought back with Alain from his travels with her gift of pigments, and a large portrait hung over the staircase. Two people in the glorious brocades of decades past, staring down at their granddaughter with astonished painted eyes.

'Who is that?' Marie asked, climbing up on a stool for a closer look.

'Those are my parents,' Françoise's voice said from a doorway. 'So they are your *grandmère* and *grandpère*. It was painted when they were young and lived in France. I think you must be Mademoiselle Marie.'

Sandrine turned to look at Alain's sister. Françoise seemed a little nervous in that moment, just as Sandrine was herself. The young woman smoothed her skirt, tucked a curl behind her ear. She watched Marie with wonder in her eyes, and a little caution.

Marie gave her a little curtsey, as Sandrine had taught her. It was pretty indeed, a graceful movement that would not have been out of place in the châteaus of those people in the portrait, and Sandrine thought she might burst with pride. 'I am Marie. How do you do, Madame?'

Françoise smiled, that sudden sunburst so similar to Alain's. She hurried forward with her hand held out, her engagement sapphire gleaming. 'And I am your *tante* Françoise. I'm so happy to meet you at last! Will you come into the drawing room? I have some caramel cakes all the way from Paris that I think you might like as much as I do.'

Marie happily took Françoise's hand and followed her, the two of them chattering about their favourite sweets. Sandrine stepped closer to Alain and whispered, 'I hope your sister was happy when you told her? Not too shocked? Or angry at me?'

Alain quirked a smile down at her, one she could not quite read. He was maddening that way. 'Shocked, of course. But also very excited. She does love children; she shares a delight in the world with them, a joy of little discoveries. I am sure you need have no fear of Marie being with her.'

'I do not fear it.' She did not fear Françoise, how could she? The girl had always been kind and charming, and clearly Marie already liked her. She just feared *hoping* again. The fear of hope was such a fragile, bittersweet thing, a longing so intense and shadowed by the fear that it might all slip away.

But there was only one way ahead now. Forward.

She gathered up her parcel of sketches and followed Alain towards the drawing room.

'She will love your ideas for her gown, too,' he said. 'She could find no one else to make her look so magical on her grand day.'

He sounded so sure, so confident in her skills, it gave her confidence, too. She'd dressed many brides, but somehow this one seemed the most important of all.

Marie sat on a pale yellow settee with Françoise, the two of them pouring tea and chatting as if they had known each other for years and years, had never been apart. 'Maman, Tante Françoise tells me she once had a doll called Laure, who has dark curls like me, and I might play with her later if I am very careful, for she is French.'

'That is wonderful, *petite*,' Sandrine managed to murmur, afraid she might cry. She watched Alain sit with them, watched Marie carefully pour him a cup of tea. Marie was quite like a young lady now, in this scene Sandrine had never dared to dream of before. This vision of a *family*. Bittersweet tenderness ached inside her heart, filled with longing even as it comforted her. Time was fleeting; she had this now. Could she be brave enough to find a way to hold on to it?

Françoise glanced up and smiled with delight. 'Sandrine, Alain says you have the most beautiful ideas for my gown! Shall we look at them?'

'I can help you choose the ribbons, Tante Françoise,' Marie said confidently. 'I do it all the time.'

Sandrine watched from the nursery doorway as Alain tucked the blankets around Marie, folding her in safe for the night. She had cajoled him into reading her not one but two of her storybooks, wrapping him neatly around her darling finger, but now her eyelids were heavy.

His eyes were soft, filled with wonder and pride as he watched her, as if memorising every tiny detail.

'Will we get marzipan at Mollands tomorrow?' Marie murmured.

'Yes, of course. And lemonade, too,' he said. 'But I think now it is sleepy time.'

Marie nodded, and snuggled her doll close. But as Alain rose to leave, she clutched his sleeve. 'You *will* come back?'

'I will,' he said simply, all the world in those two words.

He followed Sandrine out of the nursery and down the stairs to the drawing room, the two of them silent as she lit a lamp against the night outside. There were no words she could think of to express the depth of her feelings in that moment.

She didn't know what else to do, so she just followed her instincts. She went to him and kissed him. The taste of him, like dark chocolate, the way his mouth felt on hers, the way his body moved against hers—it sent her back and back in time, to the blurry *wanting* of their wedding night.

His hands closed over her shoulders, and for a moment she feared he might push her away. Then he groaned, a wild sound deep in his throat, and his arms closed around her to drag her to him so there was nothing between them at all.

Chapter Fifteen

The house was silent around them, the two of them seeming to be alone in the world. She wondered if this had been a mistake, if she should have kept him at a distance, but as she stared up at him after their kiss she knew it was right to be alone with Alain. To be only with him now.

'Sandrine,' he whispered roughly. 'I've missed you for so long.'

He took her face between his hands, holding her lightly, gently, as if she was a rare, precious jewel. His thumbs caressed her cheeks until she dared to look up at him, into his deep, dark eyes, and she fell into him completely. He gave her the most tender, heartbreaking smile.

'Sandrine,' he said, and there was so very much in that one word.

'Yes,' she answered simply.

His lips met hers, softly at first, as if it were their very first kiss. A beginning. When she moaned against him, he pressed deeper, the tip of his tongue tracing the curve of her trembling lower lip before he slipped inside, tasting her as if starved for only her. She felt his fingers slide into her hair, loosening it from its pins and combs, letting it tumble over her shoulders, over his arms. He held her so close, as if he feared she would escape from him.

But she never wanted to be apart from him again. She only wanted this to be real, at last, and she would even deceive herself in the moment to make it so.

He tasted so wonderful, of wine and fruit, and of that essence of only *Alain* that she craved. She reached for him, dug her fingers into his shoulders and pressed herself against him so tightly nothing could come between them.

He groaned her name against her lips, and his arms closed around her to carry them down to her chaise. Their kiss turned harder, wilder, and something she'd hidden deep inside of herself since they parted all those years ago burst free.

She shoved his coat from his shoulders and he tossed it to the ground. Her shaking fingers unbuttoned his silk waistcoat, untangled his cravat, reached for the hem of his shirt. It caught on his breeches, and they both laughed against each other.

At last, at last, she touched his lean naked chest, running a caress over the silken-warm skin, feeling his muscles tighten at her touch as their lips met in another kiss. She felt his breath against her, the sheer, vital life of him. She wanted only to feel all of him, see him, *know* him as he was now, as he truly was.

His lips slid from hers to kiss her cheek, the pulse

that beat so frantically at her temple. The sigh of his breath against her ear made her tremble. He traced a fiery ribbon of open-mouthed kisses, butterfly light, along her arched neck, and drew away the lace edge of her gown to kiss the curve of her shoulder, the sensitive swell of her breast.

'Alain,' she sighed.

As if that whisper, so filled with longing, unleashed something inside of him, he pulled hard at her gown, snapping the little pearl fastenings. Her stays, her chemise followed, his breath heavy. She lay beneath him in only her stockings, not scared or shy, but only longing.

Such a wondrous sense of *freedom* swept over her as his eyes hungrily took in every inch of her. She stretched her arms above her head and arched her body against his, enticing him back to her.

He tore off the last of his clothes, making her laugh in delight at his hunger that matched her own. He was leaner now, harder, but more handsome, more alluring, than ever. He lowered himself over her, their bodies pressed together, entwining.

His head, with its dark, tangled curls, bent towards her and his kisses were pressed, one after the other, to her breast, her waist, and up again. Until at last his mouth closed over her aching nipple, his tongue swirling expertly around its tip, his teeth catching it. Sandrine gasped, and twined her fingers in his hair to hold him against her.

She wrapped her legs around his hips as his mouth moved to her other breast, kissing, tasting, until she couldn't breathe at all, could remember nothing but him. Her eyes fluttered closed as she felt his rough palm slide over her ribs, the flare of her hip. His fingers feathered lightly over her skin, teasing, closer and closer to the aching core of her but then inching teasingly away.

Her head fell back against the cushions, a flood of heated emotions rushing over her. She arched under the delight of his hands, his mouth. She felt as if she was awakening at last. 'Please, Alain!' she sobbed. *'Maintenant!'*

With a rough laugh, he gave her what she wanted, what they both wanted. One finger slid deep inside of her, his thumb lightly brushing that one most sensitive spot.

'Do you like that, *chèrie*?' he said hoarsely, his kiss sliding over her neck again. 'Shall I touch you just— *there* again?' And there was that spot again, making her cry out. He knew her far too well.

'Yes,' she whispered, and almost sobbed at the glorious sensation only he could bring. 'Alain, please.'

His eyes watched her as if she were the only thing in all the world, his face intense, focused, pained. Suddenly, as if he could bear it no longer, his hands closed hard on her waist and he turned her over. She braced her palms on the velvet cushions and felt his hands drawing her hips up and back, under his mastery. She spread her legs further apart and cried out as he thrust into her.

Being joined with him again felt so *right*, so perfect. She arched back against him to bring him even closer.

'Sandrine,' he murmured. He held her hips and began to move, a fast, hard, hungry rhythm punctuated by their mingled harsh breaths, the slide of skin against skin. They found their pattern together, moving as one.

She closed her eyes tightly and revelled in every movement, every feeling of him against her. That hot pleasure she once remembered from their wedding night was now increased a hundredfold, gathering in a tight knot deep inside of her, expanding with every movement. She reached for it, desperate, closer, closer, until it burst and she was showered with a rain of hot, wild joy.

Behind her, Alain shouted out, and she felt his body go taut and still against her. He gave one more hard thrust, then whispered her name over and over. They tumbled off the chaise and to the floor, laughing, exhilarated.

He collapsed beside her on his back, his forearm flung over his eyes. His hair clung damply to his brow, and he looked exhausted, replete, the god Mars in repose. His free hand slid over hers, their fingers twining as they just lay there together in silence for long, perfect moments. The rest of the world was gone; worries, the past, everything floating away in that golden haze.

Alain raised her fingers to his lips and pressed a long kiss to them, the silence wrapping around them. She rested her head on his shoulder, closed her eyes, and fell into the most peaceful sleep she'd known in years and years. She was safe with him.

Alain woke into darkness, the only light starlight sparkling through the window onto Sandrine's tumble of hair. She snuggled closer to him, and he was caught by that instant of trust and tenderness, by her beauty. He couldn't bear to wake her, and he gently lifted her to carry her to the comfort of her bed. To be with her just a little longer.

He couldn't go back to sleep, even as the stars blinked on and off in the purple-blue sky beyond her window, and the moon crept higher above the sleeping roofs of Bath. The golden glow of it cast a shimmering, soft light over Sandrine's sleeping face, and he couldn't look away from her.

When she was awake, there was always a trace of wariness in her expression, a caution in her cool smile. She kept her feelings, her true thoughts, tucked safely behind her lovely face, unlike the eager girl he'd once known. And that was his fault. But now, asleep, she smiled softly in her dreams, a sweet serenity making her seem younger, freer. He wanted only to help her be that way all the time.

Her hair tumbled in a dark cloud over her pale shoulders, a rich, waving tangle, and he longed to bury his face in that rose-scented silk, be caught in her so he could never lose her again. He reached up a trembling finger to touch her cheek.

She sighed in her sleep, and nestled her cheek into

his hand, a tiny, trusting movement that made his heart stutter. He wanted only to earn her trust all the time, earn a place in her life, hers and Marie's. But how could he be worthy of them now?

She turned in her dreams, her smile flickering. She was so beautiful he couldn't bear it. He smoothed the satin blankets over her shoulders, softly kissed her forehead, and slid from the bed.

As he tugged on his shirt and breeches, he studied the chamber around him. Like the sitting room, it looked just like her, elegant and comfortable, lived-in. It was a real family home.

Leaving her peacefully sleeping, he slipped out onto the landing. The house was silent, wrapped thickly with peaceful sleep, and the air smelled of lilies and roses. He tiptoed down to explore the moonlit drawing room, the little library that held rows of leather-bound volumes, the dining room that still seemed to hold echoes of Sandrine's laughter, the lovely life she had created. He saw the art on the walls, flowerscapes that held her touch, French scenes; the jumble of dolls and hoops that were Marie's.

That house gave him such a feeling of yearning. Like her bedchamber, the whole dwelling felt like a part of her. Elegant, informal, welcoming, filled with just the art and porcelain and colours she liked. It was a true home. Alain had never had a home of his own, never even considered what one might be like. His parents' home had not even seemed to belong to them, too filled with regrets and sadness. His travels and work had taken him to a succession of rented rooms, hotels, even tents in deserts. Some shabby, some a little scary, some luxurious, but never *his*. Never a place to share, to belong. Never a place where he could be himself.

Sandrine created such spots all around her, wherever she was. Her shop, her house, every party she walked into. People gathered around her, wanted to be near her, just as he did.

He studied a portrait of Marie that hung on the wall, her laughing blue eyes, her beautiful little face, the mischievous spirit that shone out of her. Could he possibly be a good father? A real husband? How he wanted to be only that.

He closed his eyes and pictured how it might be if *he* lived in this magical little house with two beautiful ladies. If they all belonged together, with sunny days of laughter, cosy evenings by the fire. He felt such an ache of yearning, grief, regret, and a new determination. He realised in that moment that he *needed* Sandrine, as he had never needed anything else in all the world. Not just her beauty, the passionate fire of her lovemaking, but her steady intelligence, her gift for making the world peaceful and elegant, her deep *knowing*. The strength of her.

What could he give her in return? He could give her a strong base for launching all her dreams, if she would let him. He could be a partner, someone who admired and adored her beyond reason. Who saw all the beautiful things she was.

There was a soft footfall behind him, the click of a

floorboard, and he glanced over his shoulder. Sandrine stood there in the doorway, watching him carefully, cautiously. A dark velvet dressing gown was drawn around her, her dark hair in waves over her shoulders. It was the most intimate thing he had ever seen, and it was exactly what he wanted to claim, to know for the rest of his days.

'Alain?' she said softly. 'Are you all right?'

And for the first time in—well, the first time *ever*—he thought he just might be.

'I am perfect.' He held out his hand, hoping beyond hope she would take it, that he could no longer be alone. She smiled, and stepped forward to slip her hand into his. Her fingers were soft, warm, steady in his.

He nodded at the portrait. 'You have captured her spirit so perfectly.'

Her smile turned soft. 'She is a miracle. So filled with light and joy.' She paused, tilting her head to glance between him and Marie's image. 'Are you greatly angry? That I did not find a way to tell you?'

The silence between them felt tense as he struggled to make sense of his tangled emotions. 'I might have been, at first. But I know now why you didn't think you could tell me. I was so careless, so sure of myself when I was young that I ran over everyone else. And I am sorry I gave you such reason to mistrust me. My callow foolishness cost me so much time with you and Marie. I will always be angry with *myself* for that.'

She squeezed his hand in the silence after that painful confession. 'Let's go back to bed,' she said simply, and tugged at his hand to draw him with her. He'd never known such a rush of perfect happiness, such raw hope, in just that one small moment.

Chapter Sixteen

Sandrine couldn't remember the last time she'd felt so—so *bouncy* with fun before, as she fairly skipped up the stairs of her friend Penelope Oliver's house towards the waltzing party that waited there. She felt so young, so light, so free, filled with possibilities! And she feared it was quite due to Alain.

In the past few days, they'd had long walks with Marie, card games by the fire at home, like a real family. Nights of wild passion. Laughter, talk, all the years between them filled and banished. It was more than she could ever have expected.

She paused in the drawing-room doorway to smooth the waterfall-lace sleeves of her sunset-coloured gown, and study the party gathered there. She couldn't see Alain yet, and felt a tiny sting of disappointment.

She moved through the room, nodding and smiling with patrons and friends. She tried not to look for him, not to be distracted—until he really was there. She hurried towards him, and he smiled, a wide, white, eager grin. He took her hand under cover of a fold in her skirt, and seemed as eager to see her as she was him.

'Sandrine,' he murmured.

'Come with me,' she whispered. 'I know where to go.' She led him down the corridor to a small library she knew of, and as soon as the door shut behind them he seized her in his arms and kissed her, their lips meeting desperately.

Alain seized her by the waist and spun her around, making her laugh helplessly as the room twirled and dipped around them. He lifted her up onto a table, and she wrapped her arms and legs around him, her skirts a rose-coloured cloud around them. He kissed her neck, his lips so warm, so enticing on her skin. She forgot the party outside, forgot everything but him and how happy she was in that moment.

Her head fell back, and his kisses spread down her shoulder, up to nibble at her ear, all around her. A hot sensation rushed through her, and she laughed with joy.

'Alain...' she whispered. 'We'll be missed.'

'Not yet,' he murmured against her. 'Oh, Sandrine, I never want to be anywhere but here. Now.'

'Nor do I. Only with you, everywhere with you.' He dragged her closer, and she felt the press of his hardness, his desire, through her skirts. It made her even dizzier, and she kissed him again, falling into the blurry heat of it all.

Never, even in her youthful love for him so long ago, did she imagine such feelings. Such raw, burning need. She clung to him, willing herself to believe this was truly real.

'Sandrine,' he groaned. 'I want you so much. Kiss me again.'

'And again and again!' Their lips met, clashed, filled with need.

There was a creaking noise just outside the door, as if someone fell against it, and a burst of laughter. A stark reminder that there really was a world beyond their little circle, and they couldn't leave it behind just yet. Sandrine laughed, and gave Alain a playful little shove that made him stumble back from her. He laughed, that deep, warm-whiskey rumble she loved so much, and lifted her down from the table. He smoothed her skirts, only making them worse.

'Here, let me help,' he teased, and tugged her lacy sleeve down her shoulder. His head bent as if to kiss her again, and she stepped away, spinning from him even as she wanted to move closer.

'*Homme hilarant*,' she giggled. 'We can never leave if you do that!'

'That's the idea.' He gave her another kiss, longer, hotter. 'Oh, Sandrine. I didn't think I could ever be as happy as I am now. I never imagined anything like this.'

Nor had she. He looked like a god in the moonlight, alluring, beautiful. A god who watched only her, focused only on her. She seemed to teeter between bliss and worry, each feeling stabbing so sharp. Could she really be with Alain now, this time? Could she let herself have this one perfect thing, let herself believe it?

She was *happy*. Happy with Alain, happy with herself. She was *alive*. Free.

And it was thanks to him, to the bright days they'd shared together. Yet a part of her, a strong, insistent thought, like a ghost that dragged the past behind it and wouldn't leave her alone, told her this was too fragile, too beautiful, to last.

She reached up and touched his face. The roughness of his beard prickled at her palm, and his skin was warm and soft underneath. He turned his head to press a kiss into her palm.

'I am happy, too,' she whispered.

His hand covered hers, holding her with him. 'Then perhaps we could…' He hesitated, faltered, shook his head. He seemed so uncharacteristically unsure and young in that instant.

'Could what?'

'Could marry again, retake our vows. But for good this time?' he said slowly.

Sandrine was not expecting that. 'M-marry?' she muttered.

He nodded eagerly. 'Yes! Why not? We could then feel this way always, make a home, a true home, with Marie. We can be a family.'

And that was all she had ever really wanted. The younger Sandrine would have swooned away with the joy of it! The Sandrine *now* felt dizzy at the thought. Yet something held her back. Maybe it was that ghost, that old fear and hurt. The lonely nights she'd spent.

She loved Alain, loved him with all her being. She just had to be sure.

'Oh, Alain,' she whispered. 'I just need a little more time.'

He shook his head, reaching out for her. She stepped away, knowing if he touched her she would be lost. 'Have we not had too much time apart already? That was all my fault. Please, let me make it up to you. Let me give you anything you want.'

How she yearned to believe him! She swayed towards him, and he caught her against him, safe and warm and steady. But what if it changed? What if he found that once they were married, once they had made their home, their everyday lives, together, he did not want that? Did not want *her*? She had Marie to think of now. Marie to protect.

'Just give me a bit more time, Alain, please,' she said, afraid she would choke on the words, would cry in front of him.

'I would give you anything you asked, Sandrine, I promise,' he answered.

She ached to stay there, to hold on to him again, to give in and let herself believe. But she backed away, and fled from the room, so confused and lost. The light and noise of the party was a surprise after the warm intimacy of their little room, their little world of two. She blinked against it, wishing she could escape.

She heard the door open behind her, and knew Alain would soon appear beside her. She couldn't look at him, smile as if nothing had happened. It was far too tempting. She plunged ahead into the crowd, making herself laugh and chat. She glimpsed Mary and Adele, with Françoise d'Alency, and waved at them in greeting. As she moved to chat with them, a new group appeared in the drawing-room doorway from the staircase, and their hostess, Penelope Oliver, went to greet them.

'Oh!' Adele exclaimed. 'Who is that lady? I don't think I have seen her in Bath before. She is incredibly beautiful, isn't she?'

Sandrine turned to look, curious, wondering if it was someone she should entice into her shop—and froze. The lady who stood there, serenely smiling and nodding at Penelope, was Danielle Aurac. Still angelically beautiful, even in her stark black satin gown that proclaimed her a widow.

She suddenly realised exactly what had held her back when Alain declared he wanted to marry again. It was *this*. The past coming into the present, always there, always real. The chance of Alain seeing his old love again. Or was Danielle still his *real* love? Maybe she was there in Bath because of him. Had he rushed to Sandrine because he merely wanted to be free of his passion? What was it Mrs Smythe had said? Rakes did not change.

'Why, that is...' Françoise said, her voice tight. Adele glanced at her curiously. 'That is Mademoiselle Aurac. Her grandfather was Alain's schoolmaster. He used to speak of them so fondly. I had heard she married, though she must be widowed now. How strange she would be here in Bath.' Her hand landed on Sandrine's arm, in unspoken understanding.

Sandrine didn't want to be watched, for fear her careful, smiling mask would crack. 'Do excuse me for a moment, my dears,' she managed to say. She turned to leave, to find some quiet refuge, and saw Alain. He stared at Danielle, his face pale, eyes wide in shock. He seemed locked into place, unable to look away from her, to see anything else. Danielle looked back at him, leaned towards him as if she would rush to him. Sandrine felt like an interloper, a fool. Again. She spun the other way and left the party, alone.

Alain no longer felt like himself, not like the man he was now. He was shoved back into the past when he saw Danielle walking towards him, as golden and beautiful as ever. He was the Alain he'd once been, the one he thought he'd banished forever.

'*Bonjour*, Alain. It is so very good to see you again.' She positively purred the words, in that low voice he remembered so well.

Alain stared down at her, every nerve frozen, every thought gone still. How could she be there again, right before him, after all these years?

How he had once longed for her, as the lost young man he'd been! How strange it all seemed now.

He must have been silent for too long, for her gaze, her smile, flickered, and a little frown creased between her eyes. 'Alain? I do hope you remember me.'

He shook himself out of his spell, and gave her a

bow. 'How could I not? Mademoiselle Aurac. Oh, no, I know you are Madame now.' She held out her dark-gloved hand, and he had to take it, to feel that touch that had once meant everything to him. 'I am most happy to see you looking so well, though I think you might be in Bath to recover from a loss?' He gestured to her black garb.

'Yes.' She fluttered her black lace fan, studying him over its edge. 'My husband sadly departed this world a few months ago. I have been quite lost without him, and my doctor told me the waters of Bath would greatly benefit me.' She touched his sleeve. 'It is such a delightful relief to find an old friend here! The years have certainly been kind to you, Alain.' Her eyes slid over him, lower, lower. 'Most kind indeed.'

Once, her attention, her admiration, would have been all he longed for. Now, though, the frozen moment of shock at seeing her again flowed away, and he was back to himself, the Alain who was here now. The Alain who had grown, changed, learned. The one who knew what real love was.

The Alain who had just kissed Sandrine, held her in his arms. The force of his feelings for her made what he'd once known of Danielle, what he'd once thought so vital in the world, pale and pallid.

But she *had* once meant a great deal to him; her family and their school had once been his refuge. He owed her friendship, surely. Owed it to her to help her in her bereavement, if he could. Surely that was all she expected.

He smiled at her, his face feeling tight, forced, and held out his arm for her to take. 'Shall we walk for a bit? I am eager to hear how you fare, Lady Darby.'

She smiled up at him, a flash of relief, flirtation. She slid her hand over his sleeve, her fingers curling over it. 'Oh, Alain, do call me Danielle. We are such old friends, we were once so very—so very close.'

'Once, perhaps.' He glanced up to sweep a look around the party. Françoise watched him with wide, shocked eyes, but Sandrine was not there. 'Tell me, then, what besides your doctor's orders brings you to Bath? I hope you are not unwell.'

'Oh, no, my physical health is excellent. I have come to stay with friends, who have kindly extended an invitation for the rest of the winter.' She waved her fan at the group she had appeared at the party with. 'I have been a sad wanderer since my husband died, never quite sure where I should alight. Where I might belong.' A flash of sadness, almost despair, flickered over her face. They had once been such friends; Alain was worried about her now.

'You seek a new home? Perhaps one without so many memories?' he said gently.

'Exactly so, Alain. How understanding you have always been!' She squeezed his arm, smiling lightly again. 'I did love my home with my husband, his lovely estate where we were so happy together. Everyone there loved me, said I made their lives so much brighter! But my poor husband was rather older than me, and the estate went to his son and his wife, who was not so fond of the tenants and servants as I was. There was little room for me there, and, while I have a small income, there was no suitable dower house. I must wander now, and find my place again.'

'How could you fail to do so?' he said, automatically chivalrous. There were so many memories crowding in on him, of walks with Danielle, soft conversations, yearnings and hopes, and disillusionment.

She laughed. 'Dearest Alain. I am so happy to find you again! What a kind friend you always were. But then, you must know how it feels to be quite adrift. I heard you have been travelling for many years, seeing all the world.'

'Not quite all of it. I have seen some glorious sights, yes, and have been learning a great deal. Both of work and of life.' And he had learned the value of real love. If only he had seen it so much sooner.

'You have truly accomplished so much. My grandfather would be proud to see it. You were always his favourite pupil.'

'He was an excellent teacher. You must miss him.'

'Indeed. My life has never quite steadied since he left us.' She stopped, tugging at his arm to keep him by her side, staring up at him intently. 'Now it feels like those beautiful times again, seeing you here, Alain. I have missed you so much! Such regrets I have had. So much I long to say to you.'

Alain, too, was beset with regrets. He thought they were not at all the same as whatever Danielle held on to now. He only regretted losing what could have been with Sandrine.

'We are very different people from who we were then,' he said.

'They were good times. You must let me see you again, talk of it all.'

'We are talking now.'

She shook her head and slid a step closer to him. Her heady gardenia scent wrapped around them. 'Not like this. I have things I must say. I beg you, for the sake of our past. Of our possible future?'

She looked so desperate in that moment, so sad, and Alain remembered what he owed her grandfather. 'Very well. Shall we walk in Sydney Gardens tomorrow?'

'Oh, Alain. Yes. I will find you there.' She touched his sleeve again, her fingers curling into him. 'You have been a good friend.'

He had to be away from her, to listen to his wan thoughts. Fortunately, her friends came seeking her then, and Françoise came and dragged him away through the crowd.

'Here, brother, you look as if you could use this,' she said, and pressed a wine glass into his hand.

'Merci.' He took a deep swallow, and looked around for Sandrine. He was desperate to see her, to tell her what he knew now—he loved her, only her. He always had.

'She left a while ago. She did look rather pale,' Françoise said. She watched him with narrowed eyes, as if she knew. As if she was disappointed in him. 'It has become rather crowded at this party.'

Had she seen him with Danielle? Had he made a hash of things yet again? He had to make things right! 'I must find her...'

'I am sure her carriage has already departed. And really, Alain, sometimes a lady just needs a moment alone.'

He was puzzled. 'Alone for what?'

Françoise sighed and shook her head. 'Oh, Alain. Was that not Danielle Aurac you were walking with just now? What a surprise to see her here in Bath, after all this time.'

'Yes, a great surprise.'

She took his arm and walked him, marched him, around the room. 'I heard that her late husband left her in quite perilous straits. So very sad. I am sure she will find a new match soon enough.'

He studied her closely, and she smiled innocently. 'You've heard all that already?'

'I am to be a diplomat's wife! I must observe and listen to everything. Mrs Patterson over there told me, and you know she is quite the Bath gossip. I might have mentioned I used to know Danielle and was concerned. She is staying in a room at Trim Street.'

'Trim Street? She said she was with friends.' He felt a great wave of pity she should live in such an area, all alone. 'Surely her stepson would not have let her be so poorly provided for?'

Françoise shrugged. 'You would think not, of

course. But before her husband died, she lived for a time in London. Alone. And was good friends with a rather rakish earl.'

'Friends?'

'With her beauty, you would imagine she could find a duke!' Françoise spoke lightly, but watched him closely, as if she tried to read something. 'It was quite an *on dit* for a while, until her husband died and things became quiet once more. The earl married, it seems, and maybe she is seeking a smaller pool to find connections. Bath has its share of titles in the Assembly Rooms and Pump Room.'

'Françoise! How naughty you have become!' he exclaimed.

'It's only what I've heard! And she really has just come from London. I'm not sure it's true, but do be careful.'

'I am always careful.'

'Alain, I know how you once felt for her. How you were infatuated...'

'It was a long time ago when I knew her.' And he had Sandrine now.

'I was young, not blind. And also...' She leaned closer to whisper, 'I heard our parents talking of their worries. Of their hopes for your marriage.'

'Their hopes?' And what of *his* hopes? Had he destroyed them so utterly?

'I understand, Alain, I do! She was—is—so very beautiful. If the gossip is true, though, she used her husband and the earl shamefully, and now she needs someone else. Someone like you.'

'Give me some credit. I am older and wiser now.'

'Alain. Your heart is too kind. I know you like to think yourself quite hard and cynical, but it is not so. You are a romantic. You were close to Monsieur Aurac, and I know you might once have wished to be close to his granddaughter. You feel obligated to that memory. But you have Sandrine now! You must think of her. She is so splendid.'

Yes. He had Sandrine to think of now, and Marie. They had become everything to him. 'You are wrong, Françoise.'

She scowled. 'Wrong? Me?'

'Sandrine is more than splendid. She is utterly magnificent. I would never do anything to hurt her again. I did that once, and it broke my heart and soul. I have truly changed now. I see the truth.'

She patted his arm gently. 'That is true. But you really were in such close conversation with Danielle just now. It looked rather...intimate.'

He panicked at the tone of her voice. 'Did Sandrine see? What did she think?'

'I am not sure. Probably. You know how Bath enjoys its gossip. How it spreads like a flood. There are many missteps that can be made. So many ways to hurt the innocent all over again. You worry about Danielle, I know. But don't let the past ruin the present, and the future, Alain. I beg you.'

Chapter Seventeen

Danielle Aurac had returned. The woman Alain once loved had returned, was right here in Bath.

It was all Sandrine could think of as she lay awake all night, tossing in her bed. Remembering her long-ago wedding night, and the scene that she had witnessed the next morning, feeling all that hurt again. It was all she could think as she dragged herself to the shop, tried to work, to sketch, examine new fabric, lose herself in it all as she usually could.

She'd finally given up trying to concentrate, and left for a walk in Sydney Gardens, hoping the fresh air would blow away her worries. She listened to the laughter of playing children, yet it all seemed so far away.

How had the years vanished so quickly and left her that Sandrine she once had been? Hopeful, delicate, disappointed. Danielle was as beautiful as she had been back then, and she was now a widow. Alain looked so absorbed in her as they had talked in the ballroom.

He said such glorious things to Sandrine now, things she'd dared to start to believe. To long for. He loved her, wanted to marry her, be a family with her and Marie. Truth shone in his eyes, rang in his voice. In the way he made love to her, the passion they lost themselves in like a volcano. But once he'd been ready to throw everything away for Danielle. What if he was prepared to do that again?

How could she protect her heart this time? Protect Marie?

'You are being silly,' she told herself. Alain had only seen Danielle once, it seemed. She'd seen the expression on his face, thunderstruck with surprise from where she had watched across the ballroom. But had she also seen longing?

She should have stayed, spoken to him, let him into her house afterwards. Should have been brave. But she'd been too shocked, too afraid.

What would she do if he *did* declare his love for Danielle once more? If he wanted to take Marie? Sandrine feared her heart could not be mended all over again, her armour repaired. She couldn't recover from losing Alain again.

She had to talk to him. She knew that. Hear his thoughts and desires, no matter how they wounded. She just feared she didn't know how to begin. She'd dared to have hope, to picture a future with him and Marie. Seen a home. Much had changed in the years they'd spent apart. Had his heart changed, deep down inside?

She walked around a corner of the path, and glimpsed Alain far ahead, near the stone pavilion. His back was to her, but she would have recognised him anywhere, those strong shoulders, those dark curls.

The happiness of the last few days, the hope she dared to feel, made her raise her hand in a rush of happiness, start to call out to him. Then he took a small step to one side, and she saw he was not alone. Danielle was with him, staring up at him with wide, rapt eyes. Her hand rested on his arm, and he lifted her fingers for a kiss. The past came back with a roar in that instant, and she couldn't bear to see them, couldn't bear to glimpse how he still cared for Danielle. She knew she had to let him go, to be happy; there was no choice.

Sandrine's own hand fell back to her side, and she stumbled a step away, then another. Her heart seemed to seize up, to sink, and the day grew colder.

She spun around and walked away, feeling numb, as if she watched herself from a great distance. Every step felt as if she was moving away from hope, from happiness, into a future alone.

'Oh, Alain. How I have missed you,' Danielle whispered as she took another step towards him, her beautiful face tipped up to his.

Alain stared down at her, at her oval face, the shimmer of her golden hair under the edge of her black hat, her sad eyes. The man who had once thought he loved her above all else had been so young, so filled with a poetic fervour. He'd imagined so much in her. He saw now, so clearly, that that young man had been so very, very wrong.

What he longed for now, all he wanted, was Sandrine. Her laughter, her strength, her kiss. He wanted a true life. He needed her, needed what they had together. She was so much better than him, and always had been.

He longed to run to her, to hold on to her, to know what was real now. Yet as he studied Danielle, saw the desperation flicker behind her beautiful eyes, he knew that for the sake of that past, of her grandfather, he couldn't just turn from her. Something was amiss in her life, and he had to help her if he could. If he was to be a good man, a kind man who was worthy of Sandrine, he had to do that. He just could never, ever love her.

'Danielle,' he said gently. He pressed a quick kiss to her hand and laid it away from him. She looked confused, took a step back from him. 'What is wrong? What has happened with you?'

She laughed, and he heard an echo of the old Danielle she once had been, supremely confident, gliding through life like a silk scarf. It sounded so distant, an echo from a stage. The old Alain, the old doubts and fears, were gone utterly, and he knew it was Sandrine he needed. Her he loved with every inch of his being and always would. Sandrine and Marie, his bright little star—they were everything to him.

'I know that when we were young, I told you we should find a way to be together, any way we could. I longed for you to stay with me, even if we were both married to others,' she said. 'But I was so wrong then.'

He remembered that scene, too, when she had come to him after his wedding and asked him to be with her. At the time it had confused him; now he saw how young they had been, how blind. He had never imagined any feelings like the ones he had for Sandrine could exist. 'Were you?'

'Yes. I knew it once I married, once I found I loved my husband. I have always felt terrible for what I told you then, ashamed of how I behaved, and I am so glad I have this chance to tell you how sorry I am for my actions that day. True love is—it is so tender, isn't it? So warm.'

He nodded, unable to speak. Warmth and tenderness, that was what he had with Sandrine. The knowledge that they understood each other. Danielle looked so sad as she said it, he couldn't help but touch her hand, try to comfort her.

'I cannot be with my husband now, and I don't know what awaits me in this world alone,' she said. 'But you, my old, dear friend, you can have whatever you long for now. Don't let the past hold you down, as it did me.'

He kissed her hand. 'I will not. And if I can help you, be your friend...'

'You can! Go. Go to her now, and let me know there is still happiness out there.'

He backed away, suddenly knowing she was right. He knew where he really belonged at last, and forever. His steps grew faster and faster, almost running as he made his way through the streets to Sandrine's house.

His heart swelled, and he felt he was leaping into real life, real happiness, real longing for the first time ever.

Her house was quiet, still, everything he longed for hidden behind its silently watching windows. Out of breath, unable to stop smiling, stop moving, he knocked on the door, over and over, and waited to be let into the happiness of being with his wife at long last. He heard footsteps, and the whole world became brighter and clearer.

The housekeeper opened the door. Despite the fact that Alain had visited many times now, that she knew him, she frowned suspiciously. *'Oui, monsieur?'*

'Mrs Perkins, I have come to call on Madame Dumas.'

'Of course, Monsieur le Comte. Let me see if she is at home.'

To his shock, she shut the door, and Alain stared at the black-painted boards with a sense of distinct, cold disquiet.

A moment later, the door opened again and Sandrine herself appeared. She looked pale, her chestnut hair straggling from their combs. 'Alain,' she said softly. She stepped outside and closed the door behind her. Now he was certain something was very wrong. 'I am rather weary this morning.'

'Too weary to see me?' He tried so hard to smile, to pretend all was well. He reached out for her, but when she leaned away he ran his hand through his hair instead.

'Alain,' she said again, 'I cannot pretend. I saw you.

With Danielle. I know she has returned, and you must know that I—I understand.'

'You understand what?' He was desperate now to find out what was wrong, to set to rights.

'I want you to be happy, that is all,' she said. She wrapped her shawl tighter around her, as if it were a shield. 'You and Danielle weren't able to be together back then, but surely now you can? She is a widow, she can make her own decisions, and I will not bind you to me, to us, because of duty once again. I care about you too much.'

'This is not *duty*,' he growled. He wanted to shout out his love for her, show her this was real now, that it was all he wanted. But it seemed she had built high, solid walls around herself. 'I am very sorry you saw me with Danielle before I could explain, but I promise it was nothing at all. Perhaps the duty I owe is to friendship of the past, to her grandfather, but I have no foolish illusions any longer. I see her, I see my old self, for what they really are.' He gathered up every bit of his courage to let his heart show. 'It is only you that I love, Sandrine. With my whole heart.'

She stared at him wide-eyed. 'You love me?'

'Of course I do! How could I not?' He had never been so overcome by emotion before, so swept away by need and longing. 'You are everything. I love you, love you.'

Now that he had said it, let the words out into the world, he couldn't pull them back. He wanted to shout them from the very rooftops! 'I love you.'

'Oh, Alain.' Her eyes shimmered with tears. He didn't know if that was good or bad. 'How do you know? The last few days have been wonderful. A dream. But you have loved Danielle for so long. I couldn't bear it if you came to regret being with me, came to resent me.'

'It is not that way, Sandrine. Not at all!' He had to persuade her he loved only her, would for ever love only her; he knew the rest of his life depended on it. 'I am such a different person now. I see the world, see everyone in it, with so much clarity now. So much more honesty. I see exactly what I want, need. And that is you. You and Marie. My family. I want to give you and Marie everything you deserve, everything you could ever want, for the rest of our years.'

Sandrine nodded, looking at him with such pity in her eyes. Her pity was the very last thing he wanted. She gently, fleetingly touched his arm. 'I couldn't bear for you ever to feel obligated. I do understand. We cannot turn back the clock. We can't hold each other back, you and I.'

'Hold each other back?' He was utterly baffled. Surely they only propelled each other forward, into being better and better? Happier and happier? 'I want to leap forward, begin our real life, together! Sandrine, I love you. Please, let me show you.'

She smiled sadly. 'But I saw how you looked with her. You cannot waste any more time, Alain.'

No, he truly could not. He wanted every moment

with *her*. Why could she not see? How could he make her see? 'Sandrine, I beg you…'

'*Non,*' she said, and stepped back, one pace, another. There was finality in that word, in every movement. She retreated into herself, not listening. 'You must go. We can't pretend any longer. *I* will not pretend.'

He suddenly saw, with the frozen stab of an icicle, what must really be happening. 'Do you not love me? Is that why you send me away?'

She shook her head frantically. 'Alain. Please. This is not about me. I must do this. Now go, I beg you, or it will all be too difficult to bear.'

And that ice melted just a tiny bit with hope. She did not say she didn't love him. She was doing what she thought he wanted. He just had to persuade her that she was wrong. He had to reach her. 'I would do anything to make you happy, obey any command you give me. If you truly do not love me, do not want our life together, I will go. But I do not believe you.'

Those tears in her eyes sparkled and fell, and she shook her head again. 'Just go, Alain. I beg you!' She whirled away, into the house, and slammed the door.

Alain backed down the steps, staring up at the windows, desperate for one more glimpse of her. He had to find a way! He could not bear to lose her, lose the shining promise of their life. He would find a way to show his love for her forever.

Chapter Eighteen

After Alain left, Sandrine couldn't bear to stay in her house, couldn't bear for Marie to see her tears. She wandered aimlessly, knowing she couldn't go to see her friends and face their questions. She wasn't sure where she could go to be alone, to plan what she must do next, and so she walked and walked through the cold afternoon.

Every street she turned down, every step she put between herself and Alain, grew more painful. She felt as though her whole being had cracked open and was left vulnerable to every hurt. Once, she had been sure freedom was the most important thing, but had her idea of freedom only been pride? Pride that he had wounded, along with her young heart, after their wedding? Pride that kept her from admitting so much was different now?

She'd begun to dare to dream of being with Alain, for real this time. She'd been so happy, seeing Alain with Marie, laughing with him, talking to him, sharing her dreams. Making love. She'd thought *they* were happy. Had she been wrong?

Or was she wrong now? She thought of how Alain had looked on her doorstep, desperate, reaching for her, declaring his love. What if *that* was the reality now? Or was she too scared to believe it, to reach for it?

She turned a corner, and found herself near Mary Campbell's house. She suddenly longed to see a friendly face, to not be alone. Had she lost Alain forever by sending him away? Had she really been so mistaken about him and Danielle? Mary and Charles's path to happiness had not been smooth; they'd faced several bumps in their betrothal before they married. Perhaps, after all, confiding in someone now, not letting that pride hold her silent again, might help. She had to sort out her confusion, see clearly again. She hurried to the doorstep and raised the knocker before she could run away.

To her surprise, Mary herself answered. Sandrine realised she must look a wild-eyed mess, for Mary's brow creased in a concerned frown. She reached out for Sandrine's hand.

'My dear friend! Whatever is amiss, Sandrine? Oh, do come in, you must be frozen. You're shaking.'

Sandrine hadn't even noticed the cold wind, but now she found she *did* shiver. Or maybe it was her heart freezing up again? She'd been so sure she needed to let Alain go for his own happiness, but now she didn't know anything at all.

She admitted she needed distraction, needed a friend to help her shore up her resolve. Mary, so bright and happy, so understanding of human nature, thanks to her work, could do that. She followed Mary into the house, let her take her damp pelisse, her hat and gloves.

'I know I sent no note ahead, Mary; so shockingly rude of me!' She tried to smile, but she knew her desperation showed. 'I just needed to talk to a friend. I am quite turned upside-down, and have no idea what to do.'

'My dear, you have come to the right place.' Mary glanced over her shoulder at the drawing-room door, as if worried, and Sandrine realised she didn't seem really surprised to see her. Maybe she knew the whole pitiful story already.

'Perhaps you have company already,' Sandrine said. 'I'm sorry, I'll go.'

'No! No, don't. Let me help you. Heaven knows you have helped me so many times!' Mary took her hand again, her grip warm and solid, not letting her go.

But Sandrine was still unsure. She wasn't used to letting herself be seen so clearly. 'I don't want to be a bother.'

'You never, ever could. Please.'

Sandrine had to admit it *was* rather cold outside, snow starting to drift down in lacy spirals. She nodded, and followed Mary deeper into the house.

She was right that Mary was not alone. Françoise stood in the drawing room, her hands twisting together as if she was unsure. 'Oh, you do have company! I—I shall just come back…' Sandrine stammered.

'No, don't leave!' Françoise cried. She hurried forward in a flurry of pink-striped silk skirts to reach Sandrine and grab her other hand. Sandrine hadn't noticed before how much she looked like Alain, with her dark blue eyes, her dimpled smile. That smile seemed very determined just now. 'I know my brother has been very *stupide*! I can see it in your eyes. What a *duper* he can be. He is my brother and I love him, but...'

Sandrine exchanged a glance with Mary, who shrugged. 'Do come in and tell us all about it, Sandrine. We so much want to help.'

'Indeed we do,' Françoise added. She drew Sandrine deeper into the drawing room—and then promptly ran out and slammed the door. To her shock, Sandrine heard the click of a lock. It was all so quick, the work of mere seconds, and her head whirled with confusion.

'What is...? Françoise?' she called out, twisting the door handle. Stuck.

'Bonjour, Sandrine,' a voice said from the shadows of the room. No. No, no, it could not be! This couldn't be happening! She was suddenly alone in a small room with the one person from whom she'd tried to flee.

She squeezed her eyes shut for a moment, trying to calm her racing heart, to make sense of all this. When she opened them again, she was still there in that shadowy sitting room, surrounded by the scent and warmth of *him*.

She slowly turned around and found Alain sitting on a chaise longue across the room, near the windows. It seemed he'd been there for some time, for a brandy bottle sat on the table beside him along with a silver teapot, and his cravat was loosened, his greatcoat flung over a chair. His hair seemed tousled by the winter wind. He was more handsome than ever, and she felt her resolve to let him go crumbling away again.

'What are you doing here?' she managed to say.

He shrugged, and didn't look very surprised to be in this strange situation. Maybe his sister and her friends often held callers captive. 'I came here to find my sister, and in the hopes of begging advice from your friend Mrs Campbell. Also...'

'Also?'

'I was worried. I thought she could help me.'

Sandrine crossed her arms, but it didn't help her feel safer. Instead, her world seemed to teeter and sway. 'Worried about me?'

'About us. About my heart. You must know that.'

'But I sent you to be with Danielle! Your love. How could I hold you back from that? This is all quite ruining it. I want you to be happy...'

He laughed, and she scowled at him. 'Do you think this all calls for laughter? How much of Charles's brandy have you had?'

He shook his head. 'Not enough, clearly. Will you join me? And I am only laughing because you, my darlingest darling, look so determined. Because I am so very happy to see you again. Because Danielle wanted to meet with me simply to say she was sorry about what happened all those years ago, and that she hopes I can forgive her and find love. But the truth is I never felt for her as I do for you. I could not.'

Sandrine spun around and banged on the door. How

she longed to believe him, to think this was it, this was the truth! But she'd let her guard down before, and look what had happened. 'Françoise!'

'I shall let you out when you two actually behave like grown-ups and talk to one another,' Françoise called back. 'You have spent enough time being stubborn. *Maintenant!*' Her footsteps, her laughter blending with Mary's, clicked away and Sandrine knew they were alone.

She sighed, and reluctantly went to sit beside him, leaving a cushion's distance between them. 'I think I will have some of that brandy, *merci*.'

'Very wise. Once my sister gets a thought into her head, you will not get it out. Best to do as she says.' He seemed surprisingly calm as he poured her a glass and passed it to her.

Sandrine took a deep draught, and they sat there together in silence for a long moment, the weight of it growing between them.

'If you wish it, Sandrine, we can sit here for an hour in complete quiet,' he said. 'Even Françoise will have to let us out eventually; the Campbells will need their sitting room back. But if you will just give me a few minutes, if you will really listen to me, listen to what I tell you…'

But what would he say? That he'd thought about it, and really did want to run away with Danielle? 'Then what?'

'Then if you still want me to go, if your heart is truly closed to me, I will leave. I will help you get your Paris shop, but you need never speak to me again. I want only what *you* want.'

Sandrine studied him, torn between hope and fear. She just nodded, unable to speak.

'When I saw Danielle again, it only made me understand all the better that only one thing matters, and that is my love for you. That our love is what is real, our understanding for each other. Maybe I don't deserve your love after being such a fool, but I want to earn it, will do anything at all to earn it. I dread to think what would have happened to me if I hadn't found you again.'

Sandrine stared at him, overwhelmed by emotion, by longing to know everything could be set right between them at last.

He slowly, carefully took her hand, holding it as if it were a precious jewel. 'I promise, I will never, ever hurt you again, Sandrine. I will always choose us. Choose our family.'

In his face, his expression of deepest yearning, she realised that his careless charm had always covered his vulnerabilities, and she longed to tell him she saw him truly, understood him. Loved him.

'I only want you to be happy, Alain,' she said.

'How could I ever be happy without you?'

She didn't know what else to say, to do, so she leaned over and kissed him. The taste of him made her forget all else, especially when his arms came around her, dragged her closer. He groaned, a wild sound deep in his throat.

'Can you deny this now, Sandrine? Deny that this is what's real?' he said roughly. She could not, ever again. She reached up and held his face between her hands, studying every inch of him, every gleam in his eyes. She did love him, *all* of him. And wonder of wonders, he truly loved her, too.

He seemed to sense her opening up to him, her blossoming belief and renewed trust. Renewed joy. 'Marry me, Sandrine. For real this time. For only us. I will work so hard to prove myself to you, every day.'

'You don't have to prove anything to me, Alain.' And he did not. They never had to prove anything to each other now. They were together, longing for the same things, looking to the same future. 'I only wish it had not taken years for us to get here!'

'But *now* is perfect. We had to learn things, about the world, about ourselves, to be ready for this moment. Ready for this love. And now it is ours forever.' He kissed her again, everything else forgotten but the two of them together. 'Oh, Sandrine. I only want to give you and Marie everything.'

'We already have that,' she said, desperate for another kiss, another touch. 'Yes, I will marry you, Alain. For real. For always.'

He laughed, a jubilant, bright-sun sound, and kissed her again, and again. 'Shall we tell Françoise we can be let out now?'

Sandrine laughed, too, thankful that, in addition to everything else she'd been gifted, she had such a sister now who had pushed them along in their stubbornness. 'Oh, no. Not just yet. I think we have rather more kissing to do first…'

Chapter Nineteen

Sandrine stepped back to examine Françoise's gown with a critical eye. Jane and her other assistants scurried around making sure every seam, every bit of lace, was perfect. The air was filled with the scent of roses, and sunshine seemed to fill every corner.

'Can't I look?' Françoise cried. She stood very still with her back to the full-length mirror, waiting for Sandrine to tell her she could see the finished product. She almost danced in her satin slippers with eagerness.

Sandrine couldn't help but smile. The joy of the day seemed to vibrate in the very light, like music.

Françoise couldn't wait to walk down the aisle, with no sign of fear or nervousness, and her sheer happiness was so beautiful to see. And her handsome husband-to-be, whom Sandrine had met at dinner when he arrived with the special licence for his nuptials, seemed just as happy, just as eager to finally be getting married.

'Just one moment, Françoise,' she said, and adjusted the short cap sleeve, making sure its embroidered trim lay at just the right angle.

She thought of her own wedding day, which felt so

very long ago. She'd been so unsure then, so hopeful, and it had all fallen down around her. She could barely remember that girl now. Especially not on this, a very different wedding day.

'Now?' Françoise demanded.

Sandrine laughed. 'Now!'

Françoise spun around, and gasped. She was so quiet and still for a long moment that Sandrine feared she was disappointed. That the gown was not enough.

She studied it even more critically, from every angle. Created from the pale silver silk that shimmered and changed in the light, with touches of sky-blue ribbon and silver-embroidered lace, the hem flared on a ruffle and dotted with hand-painted blue flowers from the precious Marrakech pigments, it had made Sandrine think of the d'Alency family's past in Versailles, as well as the sea-goddess outlines. Was it too much? 'Is it—all right? We do have some time, we could take some of this train off here, change the shoulders...'

'Don't touch any of it,' Françoise whispered. 'It is perfection.'

'I helped with the ribbons,' Marie said from her chair by the window, where she had been tasked with keeping her pale yellow organdie bridesmaid's frock from getting creased. The sunlight shimmered on her glossy curls, bound with a wreath of rosebuds, the picture of adorableness.

'They are the best part, *chérie*,' Françoise said. 'Your work is wondrous, Sandrine! A true dream.'

Sandrine clapped her hands. She wished so much

her own day had been like this, but now she could make it so for other brides, other women. And she had remade her own life, too, to be everything she could want. It was all something to celebrate.

There was a quick knock at the door. 'Françoise! We must leave for the church soon,' Alain called.

The sound of his voice, even so impatient, made Sandrine smile. She quickly smoothed her own lapis-blue gown, and the thrill of the day overcame her.

'Come in, Alain,' Françoise sang.

He came in, watch in hand—and froze as he saw his sister there in her gown and lace veil. He looked at Sandrine, as if to say 'you did this!', and she nodded in delight. 'You look so very beautiful, Françoise. A princess! No—a queen.'

'It is all because of Sandrine and her magic,' Françoise said. 'And Marie's ribbons!' She picked up Marie from her chair and spun her around, making them both squeal with giggles.

Sandrine watched them, wondering if, at last, this was how having a real family felt. It brought such overwhelming joy, deep gratitude, and a sense of belonging she'd never had before. It felt like a quiet reassurance that she was no longer alone.

Alain reached for her hand as they watched Françoise and Marie laughing together, and she wondered if he felt the same. As if the miles, the gulf, between them had mended and strengthened. He offered his arm to her, and one to his sister, and Marie lifted her aunt's train to process to the flower-bedecked carriage. It felt like something new, and yet it was something so long wished-for that it also felt familiar. It felt like home.

Epilogue

One year later

'I just don't know. Is that shade of blue really quite right?' Sandrine murmured, tilting her head to study the elegantly gilt-edged sign being raised above the double doors to her new salon on Rue des Ursulines. Those curling, perfectly placed gold letters, surrounded by loops of painted pink ribbon: *Madame Sandrine d'Alency, Modiste*.

'Is the blue too *grey*, do you think? Maybe it should be more jade. Or seafoam? It must be *parfait*,' she added. She was about to burst with nerves. She couldn't believe this moment was real, that her dream was coming true with her husband and daughter by her side.

Alain wrapped his arm around her shoulders, and as always his nearness, his steadiness, reassured her. He had been with her every step of the journey to this beautiful salon, helping her with every detail of the business before he kissed her and carried them both into the wild joy of their marriage bed, where all her worries were forgotten. He had inspired her and helped her to see that she was ready for this. He listened, showed her what she knew she should do, encouraged her. This dream was as much his now as hers.

And it was also Marie's. She dashed in and out of the glass doors now, exclaiming over the beautiful fabrics delivered, while Jane and the vendeuses artfully arranged the displays...rainbows of ribbons, ethereal laces, sketches of the very latest designs to entice French tastes.

'I think that shade of blue is exactly right, Maman,' Marie declared. 'It's so very *French*, as Grandmère says, and it matches the draperies exactly. Just as you ordered.'

'Yes, it's all just as you demanded it should be, and quite right,' Alain said, laughing to recall all the quarrels and long discussions with workmen and architects and textile merchants. 'Nothing could be more chic.'

'We will have lines of patrons up the lane, Madame, on opening day next week,' Jane insisted.

'Which means we should go home for a good supper and an early night,' Alain said as he checked his pocket watch. 'You haven't been eating properly at all, *chérie*, and I made sure Chef has made your favourite *boeuf de velouté* tonight. You also need sleep.'

'And *tarte Tatin*?' Marie cried. 'With cream?'

'*Certainment*. Just for you.' Alain tweaked his daughter's pink hair ribbons, making her giggle.

Marie twirled around in bliss at the promise of her favourite pudding. She often declared the best thing in Paris so far was the patisseries! She dashed back into the shop as Sandrine cast one more careful glance at the sign, now fastened into place. No turning back.

'There is still so much to do,' she whispered. 'There is no time for sleep!'

Alain slanted a teasing, suggestive smile at her, and took her into his arms right there in the street. 'Who said anything about *sleeping* once we are in our bedchamber?'

She laughed, and stretched up on tiptoe to kiss her husband, to feel his lips against hers, the heat of him. She still couldn't quite believe this was her life, that she could kiss this man any time she liked. And she liked very often indeed.

All her dreams were coming true now. A glow of pinky-gold joy seemed to hover around her all the time, carrying her along with her feet above the ground, and she scarcely dared trust it was all real. Her husband, her love; her daughter, now with both her parents devoted to her; her business growing and growing, helping more women every day. And now there was Paris! For so long, she'd been fighting alone, a prisoner of the past. Now she would never be alone again.

'I can't believe it's all come true,' she whispered, taking in every inch of her new gold and cream palace. The man in her arms.

'It's come true for all of us,' he said. Before she knew what he was doing, he swept her high in his arms, making her laugh, and carried her over the threshold, as he could not when they had first married. She laughed merrily, and held on to him so tightly as the world spun happily around them.

Every hope, every dream, it was all happening, as she'd never hoped for before there was Alain. The future stretched before them now in endless promise, as they were together. It was all absolutely perfect, and she knew this time it was forever.

* * * * *

If you enjoyed this story, make sure to read the previous instalments in Amanda McCabe's Matchmakers of Bath miniseries:

The Earl's Cinderella Countess
Their Convenient Christmas Betrothal

And why not check out her other historical romances?

'A Convenient Winter Wedding'
in A Gilded Age Christmas
A Manhattan Heiress in Paris

Get up to 4 Free Books!

We'll send you 2 free books from each series you try PLUS a free Mystery Gift.

FREE Value Over **$25**

Both the **Harlequin® Historical** and **Harlequin® Romance** series feature compelling novels filled with emotion and simmering romance.

YES! Please send me 2 FREE novels from the Harlequin Historical or Harlequin Romance series and my FREE Mystery Gift (gift is worth about $10 retail). After receiving them, if I don't wish to receive any more books, I can return the shipping statement marked "cancel." If I don't cancel, I will receive 5 brand-new Harlequin Historical books every month and be billed just $6.39 each in the U.S. or $7.19 each in Canada, or 4 brand-new Harlequin Romance Larger-Print books every month and be billed just $7.19 each in the U.S. or $7.99 each in Canada, a savings of 20% off the cover price. It's quite a bargain! Shipping and handling is just 50¢ per book in the U.S. and $1.25 per book in Canada.* I understand that accepting the 2 free books and gift places me under no obligation to buy anything. I can always return a shipment and cancel at any time by calling the number below. The free books and gift are mine to keep no matter what I decide.

Choose one:
- ☐ **Harlequin Historical** (246/349 BPA G36Y)
- ☐ **Harlequin Romance Larger-Print** (119/319 BPA G36Y)
- ☐ **Or Try Both!** (246/349 & 119/319 BPA G36Z)

Name (please print)

Address   Apt. #

City   State/Province   Zip/Postal Code

Email: Please check this box ☐ if you would like to receive newsletters and promotional emails from Harlequin Enterprises ULC and its affiliates. You can unsubscribe anytime.

Mail to the Harlequin Reader Service:
IN U.S.A.: P.O. Box 1341, Buffalo, NY 14240-8531
IN CANADA: P.O. Box 603, Fort Erie, Ontario L2A 5X3

Want to explore our other series or interested in ebooks? Visit www.ReaderService.com or call 1-800-873-8635.

*Terms and prices subject to change without notice. Prices do not include sales taxes, which will be charged (if applicable) based on your state or country of residence. Canadian residents will be charged applicable taxes. Offer not valid in Quebec. This offer is limited to one order per household. Books received may not be as shown. Not valid for current subscribers to the Harlequin Historical or Harlequin Romance series. All orders subject to approval. Credit or debit balances in a customer's account(s) may be offset by any other outstanding balance owed by or to the customer. Please allow 4 to 6 weeks for delivery. Offer available while quantities last.

Your Privacy—Your information is being collected by Harlequin Enterprises ULC, operating as Harlequin Reader Service. For a complete summary of the information we collect, how we use this information and to whom it is disclosed, please visit our privacy notice located at https://corporate.harlequin.com/privacy-notice. Notice to California Residents – Under California law, you have specific rights to control and access your data. For more information on these rights and how to exercise them, visit https://corporate.harlequin.com/california-privacy. For additional information for residents of other U.S. states that provide their residents with certain rights with respect to personal data, visit https://corporate.harlequin.com/other-state-residents-privacy-rights/.

HHHRLP25